DESIGNED FOR SIN

X Rated titles from X Libris:

Other titles in the X Libris series:

DESIGNED FOR SIN

Dorothy Starr

RATED

www.xratedbooks.co.uk

An *X Libris* Book

First published in Great Britain in 2004
by X Libris

A CIP catalogue record for this book
is available from the British Library.

ISBN 0 7515 3412 9

Typeset in Palatino by
Derek Doyle & Associates, Liverpool
Printed and bound in Great Britain by
Clays Ltd, St Ives plc

X Libris
An imprint of
Time Warner Books UK
Brettenham House
Lancaster Place
London WC2E 7EN

For JM, the most beautiful template in the world

CHAPTER

1

Reading from the scrap of scented notepaper Olivia had sent her, Clover Weatherby keyed in the combination and waited for the satisfying click that meant the door had unlocked.

Clunk. There it was. She was in.

Olivia's mad, thought Clover, stark, staring mad. Giving the entry code to her home to someone she hardly knew? What if Clover had unsavoury, lowlife friends? This house was no doubt crammed with exclusive clothes and bolts of priceless fabric, on top of all the usual goodies, such as television, video, computer, artwork. A thief with the right set of wheels would think it was Christmas and his birthday rolled into one.

Clover pushed the door open and heaved in her travelling bag. Anyway, who was she to accuse anybody of being too trusting? She was the queen of naivety herself . . . At least Olivia hadn't been cheated on by her fiancé, then dumped more or less at the altar like a plain, gullible Jane in a Victorian melodrama.

With a grunt of irritation, Clover gave her loaded bag a savage kick, then hoped she hadn't broken anything. Throughout the entire journey to London, she'd told herself that from now on she wasn't going to think about her broken engagement. Or bloody, naffing Roger! She was going to concentrate on having a damn good time, and she was going to meet – and enjoy – lots and lots of men, the way scandalous Olivia was whispered to do. And what better base of operations for that endeavour than in a chic, fashionable town house, right in the centre of the most sought-after part of London? The home, moreover, of a celebrity fashion designer, who was reputed to have slept with more tasty men than Clover had had hot dinners. Clover's spirits bounced up again, even as she picked up her heavy bag once more. It didn't feel any lighter, but her heart certainly did. The past was behind her now and the only way was up.

It was still strange being here, though. Clover didn't know Olivia Foxe all that well and her invitation for Clover to stay with her had come right out of left field. The two women were cousins several times removed, but they'd only ever met fleetingly at family events, and Olivia had always talked more to Clover's mother than to her. And flirted with her father, of course . . . Clover hoped that the older woman would find her a useful job to do, fashion related, of course. She fancied something slightly glamorous but not too arduous, which required her to look good but would not tax her grey matter. She had a notion to go to college again at some time in the future, but for now, she just wanted to enjoy herself. She didn't want to be a houseguest, however, a hanger-on tolerated out of kindness, pity or as a favour.

Well, at least the place is roomy enough, thought Clover, looking around as she laboured up two winding flights of stairs, past the entrances to the shop and the workshop to the landing of Olivia's living quarters. She'd been anxious about that. Olivia lived above her business – the entrance was completely separate, via a mews courtyard to the rear of the atelier – and Clover had imagined cramped rooms, cluttered with a paraphernalia of sewing machines, tailor's dummies, patterns and swatches. But, as she wandered into the living room, she saw she needn't have worried. Up here, high over London, Olivia's apartment was spacious and beautifully decorated, a haven of peace and order away from the organised chaos Clover had imagined a fashion designer's workroom to be. In fact, it was gorgeous, and Clover's spirits bumped another notch as she looked admiringly around her.

Olivia had told her it was unlikely she'd be in when Clover arrived, and had instructed her to just make herself at home. Where to first? Bedroom, so she could dump her bag and unpack some of her crushables? Or kitchen, to make a cup of tea and chill out for a few minutes? She supposed she could leave her stuff on the landing for the time being; she could almost taste that tea, and biscuits too; she was starving.

But as soon as she put down her large and by now slightly battered bag, she frowned. Its incongruous presence made the cool, pure elegance around her look cluttered. Design was clearly everything to Olivia the couturière, and making a sow's ear out of the silk purse of her decor was not a good start. Guessing the bedrooms were probably on the next floor, or higher, Clover hoisted up her luggage and made her way along another set of stairs.

Halfway up the flight, Clover became aware of two sensations. One, that the self-conscious, manufactured harmony and tranquillity of her surroundings was making her scared to make a noise; and two, she had a distinct feeling she wasn't alone in this part of the house. There would be people working in the boutique and the design atelier below, but she sensed a presence up here too – in the flat. This feeling was reinforced when she reached the next landing – decorated in the same light, milky blue as the one below – and heard what could only be described as a groan of pleasure emanating from a partially open doorway.

Oh my God, thought Clover, easing her load to the floor. Her whole body became alert and filled with energy. Oh shit, this is it! This is what I've been waiting for!

What had she been waiting for? Evidence of the racy life Olivia was supposed to lead? Well, judging by the noises she was hearing, she'd found it. In spades!

As the sound came again, louder and hoarser this time, her every instinct told her this, whatever it was, was exactly what she'd been missing whenever Roger had touched her. The X factor, the magic that had glistened like a grail before her, just out of her reach. The only time she'd ever got close to catching it was when she was on her own, and, with a delicious, grubby, daring sensation, she'd masturbated . . .

Clover crept forward, pressing her hand against her chest. The beating of her heart was so powerful now that she could almost hear it, and she didn't want to disturb what was going on beyond that open door – because then it might stop.

There were clearly two voices now, low, husky, and conspiratorial. And there was bumping and rustling. The sound of a passionate struggle between two bodies straining against one another.

'Please . . . Oh God, Nathan, please!'

Clover recognised the voice of Olivia Foxe, her new hostess and protector, but she didn't sound like the *soignée* sophisticate who'd swanned around at family occasions looking fabulous. Her usually low and contained voice was breathy and had a pleading quality, and as she gasped there came more sounds of movement; kicking, grappling, a fist beating rhythmically against a hard surface.

Clover moved further forward, keeping her slim body as narrow as she could and parallel to the door so she could see and not be seen. She felt afraid to look but she simply couldn't stop herself.

The room beyond was a small office or workroom. A heavy wooden table was covered with fashion sketches, magazines, a clutter of pens and pencils, and a spilt rainbow of fabric swatches. It was Olivia's private haven of design inspiration, no doubt, but at that moment it was someone else who had designs on Olivia!

In front of the table, and leaning against it, were a man and a woman. And the most startling thing about the woman was that her skirt was hiked up, her pants were around her knees, and her companion's hand was jerking vigorously between her legs.

Oh my giddy aunt, thought Clover, as the woman,

unmistakably Olivia, jerked her voluptuous body, skewered on the fingers of a lusciously muscular young man, whose curly dark hair straggled down to his broad shoulders. As his arm moved like a piston, 'Nathan' sucked hungrily at Olivia's arched throat. He was wearing a thin shirt made of a white cheesecloth material and when he and Olivia rocked against the table and twisted around, Clover saw his tight denim jeans were unzipped.

What a monster! she thought, unable to look anywhere but at Nathan's phenomenal erection where it pushed through his flies and pressed against Olivia's crumpled skirt. He was masturbating her and rubbing himself against her at the same time, and Clover didn't think she'd ever even imagined anything as hot as this, much less seen it.

'Please! Oh God, Nathan . . . please!' implored Olivia again, her hand slapping convulsively against the table, as her hips worked in synchrony with her young lover's fervant fingers. 'I want to come!'

Clover wanted to come too, and she had to stop herself crying out in sympathy with Olivia when Nathan rudely withdrew his hand and wiped it casually on Olivia's strappy silk top, leaving her high, if not exactly dry, and whimpering for more.

'Christ, Ollie, you are such a slut,' he said contemptuously, moving away from her, his prick swinging rudely as he sat down on a nearby stool. Clover edged forward as far as she dare, so she could still see him. As if oblivious to the woman in front of him, Nathan began to caress his imposing length slowly and lovingly.

'Nathan . . . Nathan . . .' gasped Olivia. She was seemingly paralysed in front of him, unable to follow, or to do anything about her rucked-up skirt and her sagging panties. Clover was transfixed by Olivia's crotch, which was immaculately shaven, with just a tiny tuft of tawny hair guarding the division of her sex. Clover instantly decided that she must do something about her own pubes. She looked like an orang-utang down below compared to Olivia's immaculate trim.

'All in good time,' said Nathan, continuing to fondle himself. 'Now, take your pants right off and tuck your skirt up so it doesn't hide your snatch. I want to see every little juicy nook and cranny. Come on! Get a move on!'

Olivia jumped to obey him, and Clover could see she was panting. As Olivia hooked a finger into the elastic of her silky knickers, then tugged them down and flung them away, she licked her lips and smiled in satisfaction.

She loves it! She really loves it. She gets off on him ordering her around and humiliating her.

Clover had never played such sexual power games herself, but in a flash of insight, she could see their irresistible attraction. She could feel it too, she realised, aware that between her own legs she was probably just as wet and steamy as Olivia.

'I'm ready, Nathan,' purred Olivia. She was wearing high, strappy heels and as she spoke, she shifted her feet to make her thighs gape, exhibiting herself to her domineering young lover. Pushing forward her pelvis, she reached down and began to stroke herself.

'Don't do that, bitch! Not until I tell you to,' Nathan said sharply, continuing to do exactly what he'd just told Olivia not to.

He certainly does love himself, thought Clover, her

attention returning to Nathan and his naked penis. His erection was large – and getting larger by the second, she could swear – the angry red bulb of his glans pushing out rudely between his fingers. Clover imagined what it might be like to have him between her thighs, stretching her, making her gasp and moan and want to drive herself down hard to get the best from him.

Olivia whimpered, clenching her fists and pouting in mock disappointment. It was patently obvious that she was having the time of her life.

'Take your top off,' instructed Nathan, 'Then get your tits out of your bra. Don't take it off though, just rest them on the top so it pushes them up. Go on . . . do it!'

'But, Nathan, that's so demeaning. Please don't make me do it.' Olivia's voice was little-girly and sing-song, but her heavy breathing told an entirely different story. Was she going to come, just from Nathan's high-handed treatment? It certainly looked that way to Clover. The older woman was fuchsia pink in the face and her dark eyes were wide and glazed.

'Do it, whore!'

Olivia jumped to comply, baring her body and making herself look sleazy and available. Clover wished she was part of the game too, and that she could pull apart her own clothes and exhibit herself like a slut to the dark and stroppy Nathan.

'That's better,' he said, his fingers moving more carefully on his penis now. Clover could tell he too was near to climax, and she sensed he'd want to hold off from it as long as he could. As she watched, he pinched himself meticulously, just beneath the glans, an action Clover suspected was designed to tame his pleasure.

'Now get up on that table,' he commanded, his voice

rough as if the crisis point were looming. 'Get up, then get on your hands and knees . . . Then take your weight on one hand, reach round and stroke yourself, but don't come! If you come, I'll punish you.'

Moving awkwardly in her heels, Olivia obeyed him, climbing on to the cluttered surface and sending pens, swatches and sheets of paper flying. She didn't appear to be bothered in the least by the disruption to her work. Once aloft she knelt up, her hands slowly stroking the insides of her thighs.

'Get on your hands and knees, Ollie,' said Nathan roughly, 'You know how . . . I want you kneeling just like the horny, slutty bitch that you are.'

'But Nathan—'

'No buts!' cried Nathan, rising from his seat and grabbing hold of her to manhandle her into position.

Olivia wasn't exactly a slim woman and as she crouched, her heavy breasts swung low and her generous bottom looked even bigger and rounder when offered up and prominently displayed. Her thick chestnut hair had escaped its chignon and hung down messily around her face.

What's he going to do to her? thought Clover, mesmerised by the scene, which was out of her wildest fantasies, yet also far, far beyond them.

'Now you can bring yourself off,' murmured Nathan, running his hands over Olivia's back and buttocks, slowly massaging her pearly skin in the way a sculptor might assess malleable clay. 'But first there's just another small refinement. Where is it?'

'Where's what?' croaked Olivia, beginning to sway as she lifted one hand to touch herself.

'Don't mess about, Ollie. I know there'll be one

around her somewhere. You always have one handy.'

'In the drawer to your right.'

One what? thought Clover, dying to see.

She didn't have long to wait. A moment later, Nathan had rummaged in the drawer and produced a long, thick vibrator made of vivid cerise plastic.

Crikey, Clover mouthed to herself, another monster!

Without so much as a warning or a smear of lubricant to ease its passage, Nathan pushed the pink dildo into Olivia, right up to its hilt. The older woman groaned and rocked, welcoming it inside her and reaching around herself to feel it.

Nathan dashed her hand away. 'Oh no, you've got to hold it in the other way. Go on, grip it! Make it work. I want to see it moving while you rub yourself.'

Clover craned as far as she dare, so that she could see it too. Olivia was gasping and grunting now, rocking on one hand while the other worked incessantly between her legs. Nathan watched her closely, all the while slowly stroking himself.

Oh God, this *is* it, thought Clover again, her heart flipping and swooping, as she remembered the ordinariness and sterility of her relations with Roger. He'd never had the imagination to play games like this, and not for the first time she started to feel relieved and happy that he'd dumped her. If she'd still been with him, all this might have remained a closed book to her for ever. She moved as close to the pair of lovers as she dared.

Fortunately, Olivia and her young man were completely absorbed in each other. Clover reckoned she could probably have walked right into the room and sat down beside them and they would never even have noticed her, especially when Nathan reached over, twisted the base of the vibrator, and it began to buzz loudly.

'Oh God!' shrieked Olivia, jerking as if she'd been stuck with a cattle prod. Her breasts jiggled, her buttocks heaved, and her whole body rocked in sudden violent motion. Unmistakably climaxing, she shouted a stream of obscenities that would have graced the terraces of a football match.

Olivia's orgasm went on and on, and Nathan watched and laughed with pleasure. 'Dear God, Ollie, you should have been a pro,' he said, as his inamorata's thrashing body gradually stilled. Then, with as little warning as he'd allowed her when pushing it in, he grasped the base of the dildo and pulled it still buzzing from her body. Throwing the sticky cylinder aside, he grabbed Olivia by the hips, dragged her towards him, and with surprising gentleness, lowered her feet to the carpet, then draped her, face down, across the disorder of her worktable.

'My turn now, baby,' he muttered, and though Clover could only seen his back view, it was obvious what he was doing.

With a long, hard, sustained shove, he entered Olivia, and she cried out again, her voice a croon of happy encouragement. 'Isn't that nice?' Nathan whispered, his buttocks pushing and clenching beneath his jeans.

Unable to stop herself, Clover clasped a hand to her crotch, imagining a penis as mighty as Nathan's pushing its way into her. A penis like that would stretch a woman, might even hurt her if she were not prepared for it. Not relaxed, wet and open . . . The way Olivia so clearly was.

A moan escaped Clover's lips, but luckily it didn't matter in the slightest. Olivia Foxe's groans and shouts were easily loud enough to drown it out.

'Oh Nathan . . . Oh Nathan . . . Yes!' Olivia howled, rising to another climax scarcely moments after her last one.

It was too much for Clover. Unable to help, she slipped soundless to the floor, a fist crammed in her mouth and her other hand working furiously between her thighs.

To her own astonishment, she was sharing in Olivia's orgasm before her hostess had even set eyes on her and as pleasure engulfed her, Nathan's triumphant bellow said that he'd joined in too.

CHAPTER

2

'Clover? Can I come in?'
 Oh God, what do I do? What do I say?

At the sound of Olivia's knock, Clover shot up as if she'd been goosed, and swivelled around until she was sitting on the edge of the bed. Her heart was jumping about inside her almost as much as it had been when she'd watched Nathan teasing and tormenting Olivia and making her climax.

She could feel the blood surging into her face and she wondered how on earth she could face her hostess. It would be impossible to act normally, to behave as if she hadn't seen and heard anything . . . Olivia would know in a heartbeat, and would probably be horrified that her pervy little games had been the source of an introductory peepshow for her houseguest.

'Er . . . yes . . . come in,' Clover called, leaping to her feet, smoothing down her skirt and wishing her face wasn't so carnation pink.

13

The door swung open.

'My dear, how are you?' Olivia swept in on a cloud of a sweet, exotic perfume and slithering silk. In spite of everything, Clover found herself admiring her hostess's exquisite kimono – a confection of feather-weight eggshell pink silk, decorated with humming birds and stylised Japanese foliage. Olivia looked sumptuous, both decadent and elegant, and since the scene in the workroom, she'd restored order to her thick chestnut hair. Her chignon was sleek and smooth and pinned in place with antique tortoiseshell combs. She looked confident, relaxed and physically loose in the way only a woman who'd recently been well and truly rogered could, and as she encircled Clover in a warm and enthusiastic embrace, it was obvious she was naked beneath her robe. Clover felt the older woman's large, beautiful breasts press perkily against her, and as Olivia drew back she seemed not in the least bit phased by the fact that her neckline was gaping and one of her dark, puckered nipples was peeking out.

Clover was thunderstruck. She didn't know which way to look, and as Olivia took her by the hand and urged her to sit back down on the bed at her side, the older woman made no effort to cover herself, even though she had to be able to feel cool air on her naked skin. To make matters worse, when Olivia crossed her legs and raised one of her beautiful eyebrows questioningly, the edge of the slithery robe slipped up her thigh and settled dangerously close to her groin.

'What's the matter, dear?' Olivia reached out to take Clover's hand, her neckline gaping still further and allowing one creamy breast to swing completely free. 'Did my little show with Nathan just now embarrass you? I should have sent him away, shouldn't I? But he turned up unannounced and . . . well . . . I just couldn't resist him.' She smiled a slow, witchy smile. 'I thought I had time for just a little afternoon delight before you arrived, but unfortunately it went on much longer than I'd expected.'

Clover's face burned. God, she does know! She knows I was watching her. This can't be happening.

Olivia should have been asking her about her journey and what she thought of her room, and making all the rest of the harmless small talk a guest and hostess generally exchanged. Under normal circumstances, Olivia would be gently enquiring what Clover planned to do with her time while she was in London; instead she was casually asking whether Clover had enjoyed watching her have sex!

'Now, now, sweetheart, don't be shy,' said Olivia, reaching out to stroke Clover's hot face. Her bare breast swayed, and though she watched Clover's glance flick helplessly towards it, she made no attempt to cover herself, 'I know you watched us . . . I heard your footsteps, and your little gasps once or twice.' She paused, her fingers curving delicately against the slope of Clover's cheek. 'You were masturbating while you watched us, weren't you, Clover? Now, come on, don't be embarrassed, it's perfectly natural. I'd think there was something wrong with you if you didn't.'

Clover tried to look away, but with gentle yet implacable force, the older woman made her look her in the eye. Olivia's lips were parted and they were rosy and moist as if she'd made them ready to be kissed. Maybe she had?

A deep, dark thrill of fresh desire coursed through Clover. Oh Christ, was Olivia bisexual? Her head seemed to go light and float. And if she is, thought Clover, does she want me? Can *I* want her?

'Did you masturbate, Clover?' Olivia's voice was suddenly firmer, more stern, and the wicked excitement low in Clover's belly thickened and curdled. She wanted to masturbate right now, she realised suddenly, and it didn't seem to matter that Olivia was watching her closely.

How would it be if she pulled up her skirt and slid her fingers inside her panties, in front of this beautiful older woman whom she hardly knew? It seemed preposterous, like something out of a blue movie, but at the same time, almost painfully irresistible.

Clover shifted on the bed. She felt uncomfortable between her legs again, her sex lips heavy and engorged. She *did* want to touch herself, oh how she wanted to! It was like a dream . . .

'Yes. Yes, I did,' she said, listening to the croaky sound of her own voice as if she were hearing that of a total stranger. A horny stranger at that . . . She felt a compelling urge to elaborate, to make up some bizarre variation or perversion, just to please Oliva. 'I rubbed myself through my clothes. I didn't actually touch myself, but I did come!' she finished with a flourish, feeling unaccountably pleased with herself, liberated for the first time in ages.

'Oh, well done, sweetheart!' Before Clover could react, Olivia leaned over and kissed her on the mouth. A full kiss, not just a silly, social kiss, her tongue pressing gently between Clover's lips. She tasted sweet and minty, and Clover let herself be pillaged for a moment, as the older woman explored and played gently but skilfully with Clover's tongue.

Then she drew back, leaving Clover gasping – and even more aroused.

'Oh dear, I must behave myself,' Olivia said cheerfully. 'Mustn't expect too much too soon, must I? Especially as I have to go out now and won't have time to finish what I've started.' Her beautiful eyes sparkled with blatant lust and merriment. 'Come along, dear, I'll show you where everything is,' she said lightly, leaping to her feet and artlessly, or artfully, allowing her robe to fall open. As before, she made no attempt to cover herself, or re-tie her sash, and as she led Clover from the room by the hand, she treated her to another amazing show of flashing thighs, trimmed pubis, and jiggling, swaying breasts.

I wonder what Olivia's doing now? thought Clover, some time later, as she sipped her wine and wandered around the palatial flat. Her hostess had gone out in a tearing hurry to her mysterious appointment, dressed to kill in a chic suit of her own design, the highest fuck-me heels Clover had ever seen, and even a jaunty little hat and veil atop her coiffed hair. It didn't look like the sort of outfit for an evening date in a restaurant, or nightclub, but who knew the sort of circles Olivia moved in?

Not that Clover felt entirely neglected. She'd been left with a delicious ready prepared meal that only needed heating up, access to as much wine as she wanted, and to television and DVD. Her room was spacious, quite glam, but also homey, and complete with en suite bathroom and every possible bath oil, body cream and luxury beauty product she could possibly want. She was comfortable and cosy in her pyjamas and dressing gown, she was well fed and feeling a nice buzz from good white wine, and there were a variety of entertainment options.

So why did she feel restless, dissatisfied and far more than a little horny?

Oh Olivia, you and your stud, what have you done to me?

Clover couldn't stop thinking about what she'd seen that afternoon. It would have been mind-boggling enough even if she'd been getting regular sex, but she wasn't and the last time she had, it'd been useless. Seeing Olivia playing her kinky little games with Nathan had primed a need Clover had been suppressing for far too long. She wanted erotic excitement, and she wanted a partner – or partners – with imagination, staying power, and probably a dark side, like the arrogant but foxy Nathan.

As Clover wandered into the soft-lit sitting room, a wicked notion occurred to her. There was nothing to stop her masturbating again, right here in the elegant, refined room. In fact, there would be even more of a thrill in doing it in such posh surroundings. And God knew, Olivia would approve.

Masturbation seemed almost *de rigeur* here. When the older woman had taken a phone call, while she was showing Clover around, she'd begun to touch herself during the conversation, her voice low and throaty while she clearly flirted with the party on the other end of the line. Clover had looked away at first, but then found herself irresistibly drawn. Olivia's fingertip had circled around her nipple as she'd chatted and giggled. Her hips had begun to rock in a hypnotic rhythm, and whoever was calling had clearly been aware of what had been going on, because Olivia had blithely told them she was horny, and needed to come!

'Just an old friend,' she'd said afterwards, yet made no reference to her outrageous revelation.

And now Clover was alone, and her head was filled with vivid, shocking images. She sank down on to the sofa and set aside her glass on the long, low coffee table. Half-heartedly, she cupped her crotch, but turned on as she was, she suddenly didn't know what to do. It'd been easy when she'd been watching Olivia and Nathan; she'd been swept along on their tide of lust. But now she seemed to need a specific inspiration. She reached for a magazine from amongst the pile of *Vogues*, *Marie-Claires*, *Elles* and other glossies.

Moda Uomo. Men's fashion. Just the thing. A sumptuous magazine full of the handsomest faces and the fittest, sexiest bodies on the fashion scene.

Clover flicked through the pages, glancing at dark, wild child men; groomed, hard-faced Germanic types; and long-haired Latinos, much like Nathan the super-stud. But as fit and muscular as they looked, none of these seemed to be the trigger Clover was looking for. Then she turned a page, and discovered a photo spread entitled 'Urban Vampire', image after image of cool, sharp, mainly black clothing – all modelled by the same astounding, god-like man.

Oh yes, baby, I should have known you'd do the business, thought Clover, smiling and reaching for the button of her pyjama trousers.

The tall, lean blond wasn't unknown to Clover. He was Lukas – probably the best-known, highest-paid and most sought-after male supermodel in the business. His white-gold hair, sapphire-blue eyes and knife-like cheekbones frequently graced the pages of all prestige glossies, and his spectacular, sculptured torso made him the poster-boy for a million pubescent girls, not to mention those who were old enough to know better. Clover had to admit that it wasn't the first time she'd wondered what it was like to have sex with this glorious, unattainable man.

And not just have sex . . .

The perverse nature of Olivia's games with Nathan came winging back into Clover's imagination. She pictured Lukas's cool cobalt eyes upon her as she masturbated on Olivia's worktable. Lying on her back, her skirt round her waist, she would afford him a perfect view of her sex, and her finger moving raggedly on her clitoris.

Or maybe she'd crouch like a little doggy and allow him to push a vibrator into her. And not just between her folds. She had a sudden flash vision of him putting it somewhere else, introducing it slowly, remorselessly into her bottom.

Oh! Oh God! A ripple of sensation – a tiny, mini-orgasm perhaps? – fluttered through the quick of her belly and made her clitoris jump even though she'd done nothing more than press the heel of hand between her legs. On the screen of her mind, she seemed to see Lukas raise an eyebrow, give her a sardonic half-smile, and the shiver of pleasure came again, low and subversive. When she reached for the magazine, his blue eyes challenged her, as if he'd seen what she'd been doing and mysteriously monitored her body's responses.

Shocked, Clover reached for her wine and drank deeply. Had she always been waiting to discover this kinky side of her nature? It seemed so. The thought of plain old common or garden intercourse with Roger or anybody else made her want to yawn. But how could she learn more? See more? Experience more? She knew Olivia could tell her, but could she summon up the bottle to ask her hostess outright? Or would she have to approach the subject with more finesse?

Placing *Moda Uomo* to one side so she could sneak it away to her room and enjoy it again later, Clover flipped idly through some of the other mags, then threw them aside too. Beneath lay a number of large and intriguing looking coffee table books, each with plain, unmarked covers in rich, jewel colours.

And again Clover realised she'd found exactly what she was looking for.

The book she opened first was an art book, but like no other she'd ever seen before. Appearing almost three-dimensional on the first glossy page, and so lushly drawn that she could almost feel the heat of it, was an image of a woman's naked bottom and thighs. Her face unseen, the woman was bent over a trestle of some kind, perhaps fastened there, perhaps not, but the most striking thing of all were the thin red marks across the plump, white rounds of her rear.

Someone's beaten her, thought Clover, shifting her own bottom against the soft velour of the sofa. Between her legs, she felt again that faint, excited twitch in her clitoris, as if it recognised an erotic truth almost before her brain did. Running a fingertip over the exquisitely rendered weals and then down into the intense, graphic detail of the woman's painted labia, she gasped aloud as if it were her own flesh she were touching.

What would that feel like?

Corporal punishment had been banished long before Clover had even started school, and her parents had always been liberal, but she did faintly remember certain games played in seclusion with her pre-adolescent friends. They'd bared their bottoms, and hit each other with their school rulers. It had hurt, she remembered, but there'd been another sensation, a kind of tension and excitement she'd been at a loss to understand then, but now comprehended. Punishment brought pain, but it was also sexy.

Olivia must do this, Clover thought, her heart beating faster and her belly growing tight and heavy as she turned the pages. The images were marvellously drawn and diverse, a world where pain and pleasure mixed.

A woman lay on her back on a four-poster bed, her legs drawn up high and widely apart, exhibiting her entire genital area, while another woman thrashed her inner thighs with a white cane, which looked cruelly thin and whippy.

In another image, a woman whose large, fleshy bottom was already so crimson it almost seemed to pulsate off the page, was being roughly taken over a table by a naked man wearing a mask. The woman wore a black, laced corset that compressed her waist to such a degree she must have had extreme difficulty breathing, and the man wasn't pushing into her sex, but into the tight, forbidden entrance to her bottom.

Oh God!

Oh God, oh God, oh God!

Letting the book drop, Clover wrenched off her pyjamas and began to rub and rub at herself.

'So, what have you to tell us about your new houseguest?' said a cool, clear voice, and at the sound of it, Olivia almost came.

Why did he always affect her like that? Even in far less compromising situations than this, he always seemed to get to her.

'Well, Olivia?' Francis prompted. 'You were going to tell us about Clover.'

Olivia swayed on her high heels. They were the highest she had, and awkward to balance on. Especially when her hands were cuffed behind her back and her knickers were pulled down around her knees. But just thinking about *that* made her crotch begin to moisten, and she felt the slow drip of arousal trickle down her leg.

'She's very pretty,' Olivia said truthfully, imagining Clover's delicate features, her sensuous mouth, and the lovely sheen on her natural blond hair, 'And she has a good body on her, what I could see of it.'

Would that please Francis? she wondered, looking across at her old friend, where he sat in his deep leather armchair, as relaxed as she was sexually tense and uncomfortable. His hawkish features were composed, almost disinterested, but she knew that beneath his façade, he was thoroughly enjoying himself. He always did when he had a beautiful woman – or man – at his mercy. And when they were shamed before others, he found it an even greater pleasure. Olivia glanced around the room, at the assembled group, and saw that most of the faces were far less impassive than Francis's. They

23

were enjoying her exposure, and not afraid to show it.

Olivia was in a display mode. Her jacket had been unbuttoned to her midriff, and her breasts rudely scooped out of her brassiere, pushed up and prominent. Below, her tight skirt had been bunched up around her waist, and pinned back and front, and her stretch lace panties had been pulled down and left around her knees.

It was meant to shame her, but Olivia enjoyed being presented even more than her audience enjoyed seeing her. Adjusting her stance again, she tried to give some ease to the heavy ache of engorgement between her legs. Being shown off like this was an exquisite turn-on, and she desperately needed to come. But she knew that wouldn't happen for a while yet, and she would have to stand here, ignominiously exposed, and endure.

'Don't you think you should have tried a bit harder to see her body?' Francis said, withdrawing a packet of thin, black cheroots from his pocket and slowly and meticulously lighting one. Olivia's sex clenched at the sight of it. Francis smoked very sparingly, but, when he was planning to particularly enjoy himself, he occasionally indulged. Which must mean she was in for a heavy, prolonged session.

'Yes. Yes, I should,' she answered in a small voice. 'I'll make more of an effort when I get home. Perhaps I could catch her bathing? Or changing her clothes?'

'Yes, perhaps you could.' Francis grinned narrowly and made a slight gesture to the tall, blond man leaning elegantly against the mantelpiece.

So it was to be Lukas tonight, thought Olivia. He was very good, very experienced, although she could still remember a time when he'd been a novice and new to the association. The breathtaking supermodel had always been attuned to the games though, even when he'd been in the earliest stages of learning them. Something in his crystal blue eyes said he'd been born with an understanding of the dynamics of pain and pleasure.

Before she had time to think further, Lukas had his hand between her legs and three fingers jammed roughly in her channel. Olivia gasped and rose on her toes, her flesh spasming around him already. Lukas gave her a slight smile and jerked his wrist, working her harder.

Close to coming, Olivia moaned shamelessly and looked around at the assembled company again.

Francis looked pleased by her lack of control, probably because it would mean a sterner punishment. Circe, beautiful and dangerous in a black leather catsuit, looked just as delighted. Maybe she was hoping that she too would get a chance to inflict pain? The other assembled members, around half a dozen, all looked eager to enjoy the forthcoming show.

Only Nathan was sulky. He was frowning and fidgeting, tapping his fingers on the arm of his chair. Olivia knew that he was jealous and displeased that Lukas had been chosen to do the honours. Oh, you're so naive, little boy, thought Olivia, writhing and twisting, as Lukas slyly thumbed her clit. Nathan was still new to all this, and had more to learn than he could possibly imagine – despite the fact that he believed he already knew it all. Olivia relished the fact he would soon get his comeuppance. She hoped that Francis would allow her to do his training and imagined the shock and fear on her young lover's face when the truth of his status was finally revealed to him.

'Enough of that, dear boy,' said Francis, sounding genuinely happy. 'We don't want her to come just yet, do we? She has to earn it.'

Lukas's tapered fingers withdrew and, for the hell of it, Olivia whimpered in protest.

'If she's so anxious to be filled, perhaps we should oblige?' suggested Circe, her dainty tongue flicking out over her crimson-painted lips.

'An excellent suggestion,' agreed Francis, gesturing again to Lukas.

Needing no further prompting, the blond strode to a small, lacquered cabinet that stood to one side, then opened it, reached in, and drew out an object he didn't allow Olivia to see. The next thing she knew, Circe and one of the male guests, whom Olivia didn't know, had grabbed hold of her, the man taking the opportunity to grope and pinch Olivia's naked breasts as he restrained her. Pushing her panties down to her ankles, Lukas used one hand to draw her knees apart, and with the other, his left, he started to introduce a cold, hard object between her legs.

Olivia squirmed, knowing what it was, and wanting it, yet fearing it also. But Lukas was merciless, and the heavy porcelain egg was pushed high into her vagina, its pink satin cord dangling between her slippery labia and her naked upper thighs.

'Oh no!' she keened, churning her bottom, then gasping, as the hard egg jostled all kinds of nerve endings. 'It's far too big! I can't bear it!' She tried to wriggle again, in the hopes that motion of the foreign body inside her would make her come, but Circe nipped her bare bottom and hissed in her ear.

'Be glad it's not in your arse, Ollie,' the beautiful

brunette said softly. 'Perhaps I'll suggest that to Francis once your bottom's nice and raw.'

'Enough of this!'

Francis's voice cut across the moment.

'Prepare her,' he instructed, 'Bring another chair. Place it where we can all see her. Then you may begin, Lukas. Use your belt, I think, and use it hard because her behaviour has been appalling this evening.'

It's going to get even more appalling soon, thought Olivia, panting at the way the egg rocked inside her as she was pushed into position over a leather armchair and one leg disentangled from her panties so her thighs could be spread wide.

She heard the snick of Lukas's black leather belt as he slid it from the loops of his jeans, and thought how appalling *that* would feel when it impacted at high speed against her bottom. Circe was arranging her, spreading her legs even wider to create a maximum target area. She felt the brunette's fingertip press teasingly against her anus and a ripple of shameful pleasure seemed to wind itself around the egg and pull on the root of her clitoris. At this rate she was going to come the instant the first lash of the belt seared her flesh . . .

Giving Olivia a kiss on the cheek, Circe withdrew, and a second later, there came a split-second whistling sound, as flying leather cut the air in its path . . .

Then the world went white, and Olivia screamed, not knowing whether it was from the pain or from the most exquisite, wrenching pleasure.

CHAPTER

3

The next day proved to be another revelatory one for Clover, but not, she suspected, for the reasons most people would have expected.

She'd slept heavily after her sexcapades with the coffee table books. The graphic volumes had exerted such a hold on her that even after masturbating once, she'd just had to return to them again and again, revisiting images that continued to turn her on. It was like a form of madness. She hadn't been able to stop herself.

The second book had been even more extreme than the first, and the pictures in it acted on her system like a drug. A powerful aphrodisiac to be exact. The more she looked at naked, punished bottoms, complicated systems of bondage and perverted unnatural penetrations, the more the pit of her belly ached and the wetter and wetter her sex became. It was lust in a way she'd never felt before; certainly not a bit like the mild tingle she'd occasionally felt when she fancied a handsome man. Although she did admit that when she'd ogled that photo spread of Lukas, he'd definitely had an effect on her. When she'd thought about Roger, there'd never even been a twinge . . .

But looking at the fetish pictures, she'd found herself playing with herself time after time, thrashing and grunting in a series of increasingly desperate orgasms. In the end, she'd had to snap closed the book and force herself to go to her room by sheer effort of willpower. It had been the small hours of the morning, and Olivia could have returned at any moment. Not to mention the fact that Clover had been afraid she'd make her clitoris sore and have to give up playing with herself for while. And she couldn't face that. Not now. Not now she *knew* . . .

In the morning, Clover had barely been able to look at Olivia for fear of giving herself away. She felt as if she had a huge M for Masturbator tattooed on her forehead, and that her night of debauchery was self-evident to anyone who even glanced at her. Olivia looked a little worse for wear herself, but that didn't make Clover feel better about her own over-indulgence.

So, what on earth had Olivia been up to?

It had been around 3 a.m. when Clover had finally turned in, and there'd still been no sign of Olivia. And now the older woman had a definite quality of fragility about her, combined, illogically enough, with the distinct and unmistakable glow of a well-satisfied woman. She's orgasmed out too, thought Clover, owning up to the fact that it takes one to know one.

Olivia had pronounced lavender shadows beneath her beautiful eyes and her full mouth looked unnaturally red and tender, as if she'd been kissed violently and for a very long time.

Maybe she was, thought Clover, and touched her own lips. The lucky bitch! I wonder who it was?

Speculations about what her hostess had been doing, and where she'd spent half the night, filled her mind later when she was supposed to be learning about Olivia's fashion business.

Her hostess's work was undoubtedly exciting and glamorous. During the course of her day in the atelier, Clover was allowed to handle the most breathtakingly beautiful and costly fabrics. She saw the process of design from Olivia's first scrappy sketches in felt-tip pen, to the next stage, the mock-up of the garment in calico – called the *toile* – right through to the gorgeous finished article, ready for the client. Clover was even let loose in the boutique for a while, where she pretended to dust, and tidy up, while the highly trained sales staff, or *vendeuses*, coaxed women with more money than sense into spending thousands on a suit or a dress they'd probably wear just once.

It was a glitzy and alluring world, and Clover hoped that while she was in London she might be able to become a part of it, and help Olivia somehow, although in what capacity, she didn't know.

But all the time she was in the atelier with the fabric, the seamstresses and the colourful chaos, and in the boutique with the *vendeuses*, the groomed clients and their ludicrous wealth, Clover was aware of one very significant fact. Devoted to fashion as Olivia was, it wasn't the *whole* of her life, not by a long shot.

On the face of things, Olivia was an artist and a professional, dedicated to the creation of beautiful clothes, but from time to time, Clover got the impression that dresses and suits were the last things on her mind. A dreamy, hungry expression would appear on her hostess's face, as if she were thinking about a world unconnected with fashion. Once, when Olivia obviously didn't realise she was being observed, Clover saw the older woman close her eyes, press her fingers to her crotch and sigh.

Oh, my God, she's still horny! thought Clover, her own hormones surging in response. All the time she's supposed to be working, she keeps thinking about something sexual, and it's such a huge turn-on that she actually has to touch herself. Is it something from last night? Is it Nathan? Or is it both?

By mid-afternoon, Olivia seemed so restless and distracted she barely seemed able to concentrate at all. It came as no surprise when she lost patience with a gown she was working on and ripped the entire calico *toile* off the tailor's dummy and flung it to the floor.

'This is garbage!' she cried, 'I can't bear it. I've had enough! I'll try again tomorrow.'

With that, she swept from the atelier, leaving matters in the hands of her design assistant, office manager and other staff. This was clearly not a rare occurrence, and Clover noticed Silvana, the chief design assistant, roll her eyes as Olivia disappeared from the room.

Clover dithered. Should she stay or follow? She supposed she was meant to be a companion to her hostess while she was here, so she rose from the stool she'd been perched on and trotted after Olivia.

'Come on, Clover, time to let our hair down,' the older woman said when they were alone in the flat. A few moments later, she'd opened a bottle of wine, grabbed a couple of glasses and was leading Clover into the sitting room.

The first things Clover set eyes on were the coffee table books. One of them still lay open at a jaw-droppingly perverted page, even though she could have sworn that she'd closed them and left them in a neat pile when she'd finally had to give in and go to bed. The rest of the room was immaculate, which meant Olivia's cleaner had obviously been in and tidied up, straightened the chairs and plumped the cushions. So why were the erotic books were deliberately left open and all over the place?

'Do you like these books?' asked Olivia, nodding to the open page. A naked woman was strapped across a trestle and a man in a shiny leather hood was beating her with what looked like a riding crop. The man was wearing leather trousers too, and his erect penis protruded shockingly from between his flies. He was holding himself in his right hand while he beat the living daylights out of the woman with his left.

'Um ... they're very unusual,' evaded Clover. Her hostess lowered herself very gingerly on to the sofa. Clover had noticed several times during the morning that Olivia was moving as if she were uncomfortable or hurt. At first she'd thought she was imagining things, or that it was something to do with Olivia being randy, but as her hostess gasped when she made contact with the soft upholstery, it was obvious that there was really something wrong.

'Are you all right, Olivia?' Clover asked nervously.

Olivia winced and bit her lip as she shifted in her seat. 'I'm fine,' she said, pressing herself downwards and catching her breath again. 'In fact I'm more than fine. But what about you, my pet? What do you really think of those books? Do they arouse you?'

Clover went pink. How could she tell Olivia about what the books had made her do? It was nerve-racking enough dealing with her hostess's blatant eroticism, without owning up to the fact that she was turning into some kind of sex fiend herself. Maybe when she'd been here a while it might be possible to own up, but it was only her second day, and it was far too soon to share.

'Come on, my sweet, sit down here beside me,' encouraged Olivia, patting the sofa. Clover took the indicated space, trying not to sit too close, or to appear that she was keeping her distance.

Olivia took a sip of her wine and gave Clover a long, searching look. 'Obviously the books do turn you on, or you wouldn't be blushing.' She set down her glass. 'They certainly arouse me . . . every time I look at them.' Still holding Clover's eyes, she slid down the zip of her chic beige trousers and thrust her hand inside, burrowing into the white lace panties that were visible in the gap. 'Why don't you masturbate, Clover? I know you want to.' Her hidden fingers began to move in a stately rhythm.

Clover's heart pounded. She longed to follow Olivia's example, but she just couldn't. Even so, she felt herself grow wet and slippery between her legs.

'You're not inhibited, are you, darling?' Olivia kept her gaze locked squarely on Clover, even though she was beginning to move now, and her breathing was rough. Every so often, she gave a little gasp that could have been pain or pleasure, and Clover had the strangest feeling that it was actually a bit of both.

'I . . . um . . . I don't think so,' said Clover, reaching for her wine and taking a long gulp. 'I have sex . . . I mean, I had it, before Roger and I split up. It's just I'm not used to . . . to things like that,' she nodded to the image of the spreadeagled woman and the rampant man beating her, 'or . . . um . . . touching myself in front of someone else.'

But she wanted to. Oh, how she wanted to!

'Didn't Roger want to spank you or watch you bring yourself off?' Olivia was panting now, and her fingers were moving faster, but still she pinned Clover with her eyes.

Roger hadn't wanted to do anything interesting, Clover thought savagely. That's probably why he dumped me, because I showed a bit of enthusiasm, tried to get myself off by moving about too much. He probably didn't think I was ladylike enough for him. In his book, I should have kept dead still and thought of England.

'No, he didn't. He was boring,' she said defiantly. 'I'm glad we split up now. I was hurt when he dumped me, but not any more. I want to have some fun in bed . . . I want to do . . . do things!' she finished awkwardly, realising she was as good as challenging Olivia to lead her on . . . to . . . whatever . . .

'Bravo, my dear,' gasped the older woman, her eyes glazed now, and her bottom thumping against the settee, 'Now what you need is to celebrate . . . celebrate your liberation . . . Oh . . . oh God . . . Oh oh oh!'

Olivia went rigid, her heels scraping against the carpet and her pelvis jerking wildly. She was coming, and coming hard, and Clover was transfixed. This was even more arousing than the stolen escapade yesterday with Nathan.

It took the older woman barely a moment or two to recover, but Clover snatched the opportunity to swig down more of her wine. A hefty dose of Dutch courage was in order.

'That's better. I've been dying to come all morning,' said Olivia matter-of-factly and rose to her feet. With the elegance of a former model, she kicked off her shoes, slid down her trousers then stepped out of them and kicked them aside. A second later, her flimsy g-string followed them.

She smiled at Clover. 'Why not get comfortable, my sweet?' she said, unbuttoning her short, sleeveless blouse as she spoke. Beneath it she wore a bra that had barely any cups to speak of, and her nipples were dark and puckered, pointing brazenly. Clover expected her to remove the blouse and bra, but strangely, Olivia kept them on. For some strange reason she looked more naked and tantalising with some clothes on than if she'd stripped off completely.

Clover looked down at herself, at her ordinary clothes and her untutored body. She felt embarrassed, but suddenly it wasn't the idea of undressing that made her blush. It was her ignorance and sexual naivety that bothered her.

'Don't be shy,' said Olivia coaxingly, cupping her own breast as she spoke and running her fingertip in a circle around her nipple. It seemed to be the most natural action in the world, and Clover wondered what on earth she had to lose. Not stopping to rationalise, she tugged her jersey city-top off over her head and unzipped her skirt.

'Good girl,' encouraged Olivia, licking her lips and still playing with her breast, 'You need to forget all about Roger and boring sex. There's a whole world of new experiences out there, and I can help you discover all of them. I have friends. Friends who like to play, who can teach you . . .'

Down to her pretty but serviceable bra and pants, Clover shuddered. Olivia's eyes widened, as if she'd noted the little tremor. 'I won't say that you shouldn't be afraid, Clover my love,' she said softly, 'because you should.' She squeezed her breast, then lifted the generous globe in her hand, leaned forward, stuck out her long, pointed tongue and licked her own nipple. It was the most bizarre thing Clover had yet seen, but her panties were suddenly drenched with a dewy rush of moisture. 'You *should* be afraid,' Olivia went on, pinching the teat she'd just licked, 'because fear and apprehension can be delicious pleasures in themselves. Now, come on, baby, slip off your undies. Let me see you.'

Her hands shaking, Clover obeyed. She fumbled with the catch of her bra, then almost tripped as she stepped out of her panties. There was a mortifyingly huge damp mark that stained the entire length of the cotton gusset, and when she straightened up, she saw Olivia grinning at the telling evidence of her arousal.

'You're very beautiful,' the older woman said softly, moving closer. Clover was riveted by the way Olivia's large breasts swayed as she moved, barely confined as they were by the frippery of her inadequate bra.

But when Olivia turned slightly, Clover gasped aloud. Her bottom was scored with deep red, sore-looking welts. The marks were about an inch and half wide and looked as if they'd been made by a man's belt.

'What . . . what happened to you?' stammered Clover, but in her heart she knew.

'Ah . . . the consequences of last night's pleasure,' said Olivia lightly, reaching around and pressing her fingers against her stigmata. She hissed through her teeth, but her pelvis jerked convulsively.

'What happened?' repeated Clover, hypnotised. She felt her own sex give a clench of insane longing.

Olivia looked dreamy. 'Oh, it was glorious,' she said, her voice husky, reminiscent. 'First I was exposed and humiliated – skirt up, pants down, tits out – then one of the most beautiful young men I've ever seen in my life rammed a porcelain love egg up into my vagina and beat me for twenty minutes with his belt.' She gasped, then pressed her welts again, her knees sagging for a moment. 'Then he pulled the egg out again and he and three other men fucked me over the back of an armchair, face down. I think I must have come a dozen times. At least.' Her hand slid down between her legs again, her middle finger flexing and diving between her labia.

Clover's jaw dropped. Olivia's story could have come straight from one of the coffee table books, and even though she'd always hated pain and embarrass-ment, Clover felt envious. And aroused. Desire swelled in her belly and between her legs, and she shifted her hips, trying to soothe it but knowing that was impossible.

'Was it Nathan?' she asked, her fingers itching to stray to her pussy, but still frozen at her sides. Olivia was rubbing herself furiously now, her beautiful, crimson-painted mouth open as she gasped and grunted softly, but Clover wasn't yet free enough to copy her. 'The man who beat you, was it Nathan?'

For a few moments, Olivia didn't answer and Clover could only gape as the older woman jerked her hips back and forth in a savage, almost ugly rhythm, then swore in a loud, obscene shout and went as stiff and stretched as a saint in agony, her crotch thrust forward.

Oh God, she's come again, thought Clover, longing, longing, longing to do the same. Her sex felt as if it were a mile wide, bloated with the blood of arousal, her clitoris standing proud and engorged. If only she dare touch herself, just rub a tiny little bit, she'd climax in the wink of an eye, she was sure of it. But all she could do was stand there naked ... and aching.

'No, it wasn't Nathan,' said Olivia suddenly, her voice clear and quite normal, as her dark eyes snapped open. She relaxed again and gave her crotch one last squeeze. 'Although he *was* there, and he was one of the other men who fucked me. Dear young Nathan has quite a crush on me, it seems, so he'd never miss an opportunity to get his prick inside my snatch, or anywhere else, for that matter,' she finished conversationally, as if they were discussing nothing more outrageous than the weather.

'Oh,' was all Clover could say, remembering how arrogant and domineering Nathan had seemed yesterday, in Olivia's office. Obviously there were some strange ways of showing affection in Olivia's circle of friends. Perhaps even the beating itself had been a perverted expression of love?

'Does the man who beat you have a crush on you?' she asked, watching as Olivia began to clear the books and magazines from the coffee table. What on earth was she up to?

'Lukas?' Olivia paused, setting aside a pile of magazines, but plucking one from the top, *Moda Uomo*. 'Oh no. He's fond of me in his own way, I'm sure, but he's a very cool customer, very self-contained ... He's the perfect dominant, although he's equally impressive under the lash too. He cries exquisitely when he's in a lot of pain.' Olivia flipped open the magazine, and held it out to Clover. 'This is Lukas. Isn't he beautiful? I'm sure you've heard of him.'

Lukas. The supermodel. So cool and unassailable with his perfect face and his black Urban Vampire clothing . . . For an instant, Clover imagined herself under his lash. And wanted it. Wanted any amount of pain and ignominy if a glorious man like that would fuck her afterwards.

Rapt, she stared down at the images. His blue eyes seemed to challenge her and say, 'Do you dare?' Clover glanced at Olivia, who was looking at her with a narrow, thoughtful expression, and suddenly willed the woman to make a suggestion, an invitation . . .

'Lie down on here,' Olivia said, indicating the cleared table with a graceful, enticing gesture. 'Lie down on here, my sweet and let me see to you. I can tell you want to come, and I can make it happen for you.' She smiled at Clover's look of alarm, her lips curving gently. 'Don't worry, we'll still be friends afterwards.' She chuckled softly. 'I'll respect you in the morning.' Taking Clover by the arm, she urged her towards the smooth surface of the low, polished table.

It wasn't precisely the invitation Clover had wanted, but she felt powerless to resist it. Her sex was so swollen, so heavy. She needed an orgasm more than she'd ever done in her life and it would be so sweet to just lie back and let it happen. Let someone else do the work for her, woman or not. Sex had always felt like a giant effort with Roger, for very little reward, and even masturbation involved energetic rubbing. Just once, Clover didn't want to have to strive and toil and reach.

But would the coffee table support her weight?

'Don't worry about the table,' said Olivia, obviously noticing her hesitation. 'I've had two grown men fuck each other on this. It's very sturdy.'

What men? thought Clover frantically as she allowed Olivia to guide her down on to her back on the slick surface. Her mind immediately presented her with an image of Lukas and Nathan. Who would fuck who?

'That's it, lie on your back. Bring your knees up and hold them. That's beautiful!' Olivia enthused, her warm hands easing Clover into a position of extreme and embarrassing exposure. 'A little wider, my sweet . . . Just like that. Pull your thighs wide apart, show me everything. I need plenty of room to manoeuvre down there.' She laughed again.

Something in Clover's heart, her soul, seemed to melt. She was acutely embarrassed to have the whole of her pussy – lips, clit, perineum, anus – on show, but somehow it also seemed as if she'd been waiting to show herself like this for a long, long time. Closing her eyes, she wished for a larger audience. Lukas, Nathan, even Roger, but more than that, a cast of perverted strangers, all hungry to see every detail of her wet, aroused sex, and to see it handled, manipulated, perhaps even abused. Made to come again and again.

She whimpered softly, unable to stop herself, and pulled herself even further open for the delectation of her phantom observers.

'Oh, that's beautiful, sweetheart,' cooed Olivia, and Clover could feel the older woman's warm breath on her thighs and bottom. She must be incredibly close . . . 'Francis would love to see you like this. He loves women to open their legs, to exhibit themselves when

40

they're aroused and wet and swollen, when they're so desperate they'll do absolutely anything to get an orgasm.'

Exhibit. Swollen. Desperate. Francis?

'Who's Francis?' gasped Clover, pulling herself even wider, willing Olivia to do something – anything! – and to do it soon.

'He's a friend of mine. A mentor to me, you might say. There are a group of like-minded people who all enjoy the same sort of . . . pleasures. And Francis is our leader, our master, so to speak.' She paused, and Clover leapt like a stuck pig when a slender fingertip probed the entrance to her vagina. She felt herself ripple inside, the tantalising precursor to a climax but without the satisfaction. Her aching need ramped higher and she groaned. 'I can't wait to present you to him and show him *this*!'

The finger plunged in deeper, and at the same time, other fingers pinched Clover's clitoris firmly and tugged on it.

With a wild shriek, Clover came, her channel grasping and clenching around the intruding digit and her clitoris leaping and pulsating in its delicious tormenting vice.

As her mind phased and her consciousness wavered, she imagined her 'audience' watching her and applauding, as her vulva sucked and spasmed.

CHAPTER

4

What the hell is her game? thought Clover for what must have been the hundredth time in the space of two days. Since their little interlude in the sitting room – on the coffee table and after – Olivia had said no more about her promise to 'present' Clover to her friends, which Clover found intensely frustrating and confusing.

She felt as if some kind of engine inside her had been primed, and was now revving and revving with nowhere to go. Olivia had set her running, and teased her, and then, suddenly, there was nothing; no introduction to these mysterious friends of hers, not even any more little sex games between the two of them.

After her astounding climax on the coffee table, Olivia had gathered up Clover's clothes and gently led her back to her room. Clover had half hoped that Olivia would climb into bed with her then and there, and introduce her to more of the arcane delights of lesbian lovemaking, but it hadn't happened. Olivia had given her an almost sisterly kiss on the cheek, and since then had treated her with nothing less than perfect decorum. Well, most of the time. There had been the odd kiss on the mouth, the occasional squeeze of her bottom, and once, her breast, but nothing more intimate than that. And certainly no indication that Clover was likely to be initiated into Olivia's magic circle any time in the near or distant future.

God, I wish she hadn't told me about her friends and their games, thought Clover. Because now I know it's out there, I want it!

Every time Olivia went out and left her on her own, she found herself brooding and fantasising. Where was Olivia going? Was she with her kinky chums again? And what was being done to her ... or what, maybe, was she doing to them? Clover sought solace again and again in the coffee-table books, poring over certain pages that made her feel agitated and desperate, then masturbating furiously. She stroked herself, pinched her nipples, even stuck her fingers inside herself, yet every time, even though she climaxed, there was some inner closed-off part of her that was dissatisfied. She couldn't contact that shimmering mysterious world just out of reach, and it tantalised her. Not even the selection of vibrators and other sex toys Olivia had thoughtfully stashed in her bedside drawer could do the trick. It almost seemed as if her hostess had left the various gadgets of rubber and plastic there to taunt her, to remind her of the dark and sensuous games from which she was still excluded.

It's all a ploy. She just wants to wind me up into a frenzy, decided Clover, alone in the sitting room one late afternoon when Olivia had ostensibly gone out to see a department store buyer. Clover had sensed a fabrication and believed nothing of the sort. Olivia had looked extremely sexy and very furtive when she'd left, and that didn't seem to suggest a staid business meeting. Clover had spent hours feverishly imagining Olivia in a hundred different compromising positions, being ravished by hordes of men and women alike.

Maybe she wants me to be so horny that I'll behave like an uninhibited little slut when she takes me to meet her friends?

Well, newsflash, it's working!

Sighing, Clover slipped her hand into her panties for the dozenth time that day. She glanced at the coffee table, and wondered if she dare take her clothes off and lie down on it, to try to recreate that amazing sensation of exposure and eroticism she'd experienced with Olivia. But even as she touched her slippery clitoris, she heard the sound of the flat door opening, and her hostess's voice ringing out cheerfully.

'Clover, where are you?'

Her heart thudding in time to Olivia's quick, approaching footsteps, Clover snatched her hand out of her knickers, pulled down her skirt and smoothed it anxiously.

'In here,' she answered, praying that her face wasn't too red and that she didn't smell too pungently of sex.

Olivia swept into the room, a pleased expression on her face as if she'd actually been hoping to catch Clover in some kind of sordid act. 'Are you all right, sweetheart?' she asked. Her eyes were full of a devilish amusement that said she knew exactly what had been going on and that she relished Clover's mortification.

'Fine . . . just chilling out. What do you want?'

Her hostess sank on to the settee, her beautiful breasts jiggling from the impact, and before Clover could react, Olivia had reached for her hand, raised it to her face, and sniffed it delicately. Her nose crinkled and her smile broadened.

'Would you like to go to a party tonight? You know, cocktails, a bit of social chit-chat, the chance to meet new friends?' Clover's fingers were still just inches from Olivia's smiling mouth, and for a moment she thought the older woman was about to suck the juices off them.

Does she mean *the* friends? Clover thought, watching Olivia's face carefully. The other woman moistened her red-painted lips, but her eyes were inscrutable. Was this it? Was it? Clover had to know. Then suddenly Olivia's smile widened and grew creamy and suggestive, and Clover knew that this *was* it.

'Is it formal?' she asked cautiously.

'Oh, yes, quite . . .' Olivia released Clover's hand with some reluctance. 'But I have plenty of clothes here you could borrow. I am a noted designer, after all.' She laughed softly, then leaned over and kissed Clover on the lips. The pressure was hard, almost rough, and Olivia hand's slid around the back of Clover's head, holding her in place so her mouth could be forced open, pillaged and explored. Clover half expected to be groped too, but it didn't happen. Her body felt tense and disappointed when Olivia released her.

'Don't worry, Clover my sweet, you'll get everything you've been hoping for tonight,' she said softly. 'Now come on, why don't you prepare us something to eat and I'll find you something really hot to wear.'

Flicking through her own meagre and, by London standards, very un-stylish wardrobe, Clover wondered what constituted Olivia's idea of a hot outfit. The clothes she designed for her clients were all breathtakingly sensual in character, usually involving skin-tight fit, bias-cut fabrics, and often revealingly slashed in the cleavage and leg area. She did design more sensible clothes, of course, supremely wearable suits, coat-dresses and daywear, but it was her cocktail and evening wear that had really made her name. And to Clover's mind, every Olivia Foxe evening gown she'd seen was so beyond hot it seemed about to burst into flames.

While she'd been stirring a quick pasta dish for supper, Olivia had surprised Clover at the stove and made her raise her hands above her head to be measured. The procedure that had followed had been even more titillating than their fleeting kiss. Olivia's nimble fingers had gone everywhere with their tape, recording statistics that would probably only have been useful for a made to measure wetsuit, and by the time she'd finished, Clover had been almost beside herself with frustration, and had no appetite for the food she'd just prepared.

And now Olivia had disappeared again, and the only indication of her whereabouts within the flat was the distinctive hum of her high-speed electric sewing machine.

She must be adjusting something to fit me, thought Clover. Which was awesome, really, considering that Olivia was a famous designer whose jaw-droppingly expensive clothes were much sought after by celebs and socialites. Clover wondered how much Olivia would charge a client for such a personalised service, customising an outfit at short notice. But there were other ways to pay than with money, she supposed, and at the thought of that, she felt a deep throb between her legs.

In front of the mirror, Clover assessed herself. She had a good figure, and her breasts were firm and rounded in her cream lace bra and a good deal younger and perkier looking than Olivia's. The matching panties were high cut, and what with those, and her dark, lace-topped hold-up stockings, her legs were as sexy as a centrefold's and seemed to go on for ever. She'd never be as voluptuous and downright sexy as her hostess, but she didn't look bad for an unsophisticated country girl who'd just discovered she knew next to nothing about sex.

To further vamp up her image, she'd scraped her hair up into a soft, messy topknot with trailing tendrils dangling free to frame her face. Then she'd made up her eyes with a heavier hand than usual, in a smoky look she hoped made her appear well-bedded. She'd held off on the lipstick though, waiting until she knew what colour outfit it had to complement.

'You look gorgeous, my sweet,' said Olivia from behind her, making Clover spin round, her heart lurching in surprise.

Olivia was already dressed and was stunning in a dark green, figure-hugging suit with a nipped-in waist and a rather shorter skirt than a woman her age should really have worn, although Clover had to admit her hostess did have the luscious legs for it. Especially in slim black court shoes with skyscraper, fuck-me heels.

'However,' Olivia went on, laying down garments

and shoes on the bed, and fixing Clover with a silky grin, 'pretty as they are, those undies just won't do. Put these on instead. They should fit.' With that she pressed a worryingly tiny bundle of dark red lace into Clover's hands, then stood back to watch with her head cocked on one side.

She wants me to change in front of her . . .

Dropping the red lace frippery on the bed, and fumbling with her bra straps, Clover felt annoyed and astounded at her own coyness. What on earth was the matter with her? She'd shown everything to Olivia the other night, and allowed herself to be fondled and masturbated. How could she possibly be bashful now, just taking off her underwear?

Straightening up and standing tall, Clover shucked off her bra, flung it aside, then stuck her thumbs in the waistband of her panties and skinned them down. As she stepped out of them, she kept her eyes boldly on Olivia, and received a delicate little smile of complicity in return.

'That's better. Now try the red. You'll look sensational.'

Sensational was putting it mildly. Clover contained her gasps as she wriggled into what turned out to be an even smaller amount of lace than she'd anticipated. The panties were nothing but the tiniest thong she'd ever seen – a single strand of ribbon at the back, dividing her buttocks, and at the front, a sliver of lace just a couple of inches wide. Her pubic hair rioted out abundantly on either side of it and the open weave of the lace barely hid the division of her labia. The bra was equally as racy, its underwired 'cups' just a pair narrow bands that supported the underside of each breast while leaving it completely exposed. She might as well have been naked and would probably have looked far more wholesome that way. As it was, Clover saw a porn star when she looked in the mirror again, or the very cheapest and sleaziest kind of whore. She wondered whether Olivia's underwear was just as abbreviated and sluttish beneath her shapely dark green suit.

Probably, thought Clover. The older woman's nipples were poking prominently through the fine crêpe of her jacket.

'Much better,' Olivia murmured approvingly, reaching out to adjust the fit of the red bra around Clover's breasts and giving her nipples a little tweak in the process. 'Now the suit,' she added, handing Clover an aubergine jacket and skirt in a similar silky crêpe to her own outfit.

She's chosen this fabric because it shows everything!

Clover zipped and buttoned herself into the aubergine ensemble. Her suit had a deep, rounded neckline where Olivia's had a collar with a plunging revere, but essentially the two outfits were very similar. They both fitted tight as a second skin, and, without a lining, embraced every curve and indentation of the figure. When Clover returned to the mirror again, she saw that the shape of her breasts and nipples were vividly outlined by the fine, slightly stretched fabric, and the close-fitting skirt hugged her hips and thighs, the slight roundness of her belly and even delineated the gentle bump of her pubis. When she turned around, the division of her buttocks was as plain as if the skirt had been transparent.

We look like a pair of streetwalkers, Clover thought, as Olivia moved beside her and tugged at the neckline of the suit to exhibit even more cleavage. High-class, expensive, but prostitutes nevertheless. Completely available and brazenly horny. How can I go out like this, when everybody who even glances at me can see my body as clearly as if I'm naked?

She was terrified, yet beneath her insubstantial skirt, she felt her tiny g-string grow damp.

'Shoes now,' said Olivia gaily, then helped Clover into a pair of black stilettos as high and sexy as her own. Unused to such towering shoes, Clover found that they made her stand quite differently, accentuating her breasts and bottom even more.

To complete the outfit, Olivia handed her a small, black patent clutch purse, and picked up a twin from the bed.

'Just a few essentials,' she said. 'You won't require money where we're going. Now, all that's needed is to make up your lips, my sweet.'

Ten minutes later, Clover was out on the pavement, her lips as red as flame, waiting with Olivia for the long black car that was gliding towards them through the evening traffic. She touched her fingertip to her mouth and found that no pigment came away on it. Olivia had assured her that the expensive lip-stain could withstand all the rigours the evening ahead held for them. Clover just wished she'd been a bit more forthcoming about what those rigours might be.

A uniformed driver leapt out of the limousine and held open the door for them. Clover was impressed by his courteous efficiency; that was until she caught sight of him ogling her thighs as she climbed into the back of the car. The tight-fitting skirt had ridden right up and she was terrified that her stocking tops, her abbreviated thong, and much, much more might be on show any minute. The chauffeur's salacious smirk told her he was hoping for an eyeful.

'Whose car is this?' she asked once they were settled in the luxurious back seat. There was a discreet smell of fine quality leather from the upholstery, and the air conditioning was a blessing because she was already feeling hot and bothered, despite the cheeky draughts blowing up her very short skirt.

'It belongs to Francis,' said Olivia, reclining and closing her eyes. 'It's his party we're going to, and he didn't want us to be hanging around waiting for taxis.' For a moment, she seemed to drift into a reverie, and Clover gulped when Olivia unceremoniously eased up her tight skirt and settled it around her waist, revealing a g-string just as tiny as the one Clover was wearing. 'He's really looking forward to meeting you. I've told him all about you.'

Alarm flared in Clover's heart, but, to her astonishment, she felt herself getting even wetter between her legs. It suddenly dawned on her what Olivia's sudden and lascivious display was about. She was wet too, and she didn't want to make a damp patch on the thin fabric of her skirt.

'What have you told him?' Clover demanded, trying to sit a little sideways but not managing it too well. If only she dare do what Olivia had done, but not only was she too embarrassed, she was well aware that the driver could probably see everything in his rear-view mirror. Even as she watched, he seemed to be adjusting it for that purpose.

'That you're a young, beautiful, imaginative girl and that you're interested in broadening your horizons. You

51

are, aren't you?' Olivia's eyes were challenging in the shadowed interior of the car. 'I haven't made a mistake here, have I?'

Clover swallowed. It was true, she was feeling apprehensive, but against all reason the very fear was exciting her. Her sex was very slippery now, and she feared for her skirt. Glancing toward the rear-view mirror, she caught the driver's eyes locked on the display Olivia was affording him. They were stationary at traffic lights and he was making the most of the hiatus.

The hot look on the handsome chauffeur's face gave Clover a sudden heady rush. Without stopping to think about it, she hiked up her own skirt, settling it around her waist. Her belly gleamed pale in the soft light, her tiny g-string and her almost exposed bush a dramatic contrast. She caught the driver's eye again and gave him a bold, defiant smile.

'No, you haven't made a mistake,' she said, turning to Olivia again, and her companion laughed.

'Good girl,' the older woman said, then wriggled in her seat as if she were pressing her vulva against the leather.

Maybe she is? thought Clover, tempted to do so herself. The fine, cool hide felt delicious against her bottom and the heat between her legs.

The ride was only a short one, and Clover was glad of that. With every moment that passed, she was becoming more and more excited, and the urge to touch herself was growing stronger and more demanding. It was one thing to show her excuse for a pair of panties to an unknown man, but to masturbate right here in the car? Well, that was too much for the moment. Not that it stopped Olivia, who had been fondling herself for some time, cooing and groaning with her fingers between her legs.

'We're here, ma'am,' said the chauffeur, his voice crisp, yet full of devilment. With indecent efficiency, he had the rear passenger door open while Olivia still had her hand in her g-string, but she was unfazed. She withdrew her fingers with aplomb and gave him a dazzling, provocative smile.

'Thank you for a smooth journey, Damian,' she said, allowing him to help her from the car before she'd even pulled down her skirt. As he reached for Clover's hand, the older woman unselfconsciously adjusted her clothing right there on the pavement.

Clover made sure her own skirt was well and truly in place before she stepped out, although it rode up again before her foot touched the pavement. She felt herself go red as Damian watched her closely, but a moment later they were leaving him behind and moving to the door of a select, white, stucco-clad residence. They were somewhere in Mayfair, Clover realised, but in a small private square with no one around.

Thank God for that, she thought, suddenly aware again of the tightness of her suit, and its revealing lack of lining. Her breasts, bottom, and even her crotch were a perfect picture for the delectation of passers-by.

They ascended two shallow steps and stood beneath an imposing classical portico while Olivia rang the bell. A second later, a rather archaically dressed maid answered the door and ushered them inside, pausing to take their bags before conducting them through an elegant, cream-painted hall into a reception room beyond.

The party they walked into looked completely normal. At least, it did at first . . .

Beautifully dressed people were chatting and drinking to the background of chamber music playing quietly from concealed speakers. Everyone seemed to know each other, and the conversations were animated and relaxed, an occasional laugh ringing out from above the general hum. Clover felt beyond conspicuous. She knew nobody but Olivia and she was dressed like a hooker.

But no one seemed to take any particular notice of their attire, and the handsome, smart waiter who handed them glasses of champagne didn't turn a hair – or anything else – at the sight of her nipples poking blatantly through her jacket. He simply smiled and murmured a polite, 'Good evening, ma'am.'

After a few moments looking nervously around the room, Clover realised there were other people in equally startling outfits.

Another woman was wearing a high-necked, long-sleeved latex dress, which fitted far more closely, even, than her own suit. Before she glanced away, Clover could have sworn that she actually saw the division of the woman's quim through the clinging rubber.

Then there was a man in leather trousers and waistcoat, but no shirt. He wore a leather cap too, and when he passed closer, Clover saw elaborate piercings in his nipples, and a fine chain, attached to one of them, that disappeared beneath his waistband, adjacent to his fly.

'Come along, this is boring,' said Olivia suddenly, grabbing hold of Clover and distracting her from the pierced man and the thought of what that chain might be attached to. 'Let's go upstairs and find Francis and the others.'

What others? Clover thought, as Olivia led her back

into the hall, and then up a broad staircase. Prints, or more probably original drawings, hung on the wall, and worried as she was about the shortness of her skirt, and the possibility of someone below looking up and seeing her nearly naked beneath it, Clover found herself fascinated. The ones on the lower part of the stairs were innocuous, just figures in vague, amorphous setting, but as they ascended, the images became more titillating. In one, a woman naked from the waist down was being fondled by one man while she kissed another; in another, a similar woman was touching her toes, revealing her naked bottom, while a man with his dick hanging out of his trousers pushed the neck of a bottle into her anus.

Dear God, thought Clover, faltering on the step. Her sex clenched at the thought of such a crude yet thrilling intrusion, and she felt a tiny trickle of moisture snake down her thigh. What the hell's the matter with me? How can I want *that*? It's appalling!

At the top of the staircase, they crossed a wide landing that was hung with more of the lascivious drawings. Clover dare not look too closely for fear of what she might see. Or want . .

Olivia opened a door and led her through it into another large room, once again filled with people talking and laughing and drinking. Superficially it appeared the same as the gathering below, but they were politely halted by a maid bearing a silver tray on which lay a tangle of multi-coloured fabric.

'Excuse me,' she said softly and deferentially, 'I wonder if you two ladies would be kind enough to remove your panties.' She proffered the tray, and Clover realised that the bundle was actually a heap of women's underwear.

Olivia chuckled, and immediately hiked up her skirt and tugged at her g-string. 'I suppose this is Francis's idea?' She stepped out of her undies, supremely unconcerned that she was showing her crotch to several interested parties who'd turned to observe their arrival.

'Yes, Mr Black would like all ladies present to be pantie-less this evening. For convenience.'

The soft-spoken servant didn't seem at all disconcerted by her task, or even in the least surprised by it, but to Clover's mind, the maid had seemed to relish the word 'pantie-less'. It had a rude and frisky ring to it and Clover wondered if the mysterious Mr Black's dictate applied to his waiting staff too. Was the pretty maid bare-bottomed beneath her full, black satin skirt?

'Come on, Clover, take off your panties,' encouraged Olivia, sliding her arm around Clover, and giving her not only a hug, but her nipple a surreptitious squeeze. 'Let's not keep Francis waiting . . . we might be missing something fabulous.'

As if on cue, there came the sound of a woman's voice from across the room; a high, wavering, plaintive cry that could have been a wail of pleasure or a helpless expression of pain. Clover felt her body flush with heat.

People were watching her though. At least a dozen pairs of eyes were glued to her, monitoring her every move, hungrily anticipating a glimpse of her thighs and even her pussy when she removed her knickers. Could she do it? It was all right indulging in a bit of exhibitionism with Olivia, and maybe even an insolently good-looking chauffeur . . . but in front of a room full of people? Her heart began to race, but from somewhere, she found her boldness, and easing up her skirt a little way, she reached beneath it as elegantly as she could and tugged down her g-string. She was aware that she just might have flashed her pubes to the assembled observers, but because she'd conquered her fears she felt quite jaunty. With a flourish, she tossed the scrap of red lace on to the tray.

CHAPTER

5

A second maid offered them more champagne, but this time Clover refused, even though she could have done with something to calm her nerves. She wanted her mind to be crystal clear, to see and understand everything, to know all about this strange party where women dressed like whores and left their panties at the door.

'This way,' said Olivia, grasping her arm and leading her forward, the tray of drinks ignored. Clover followed, but her eyes skittered around, taking in the elegant proportions of the room, its high ceiling with elaborate gilded mouldings, the chandeliers, the pictures, and other sumptuous old money decorations. Under other circumstances she would have loved to explore this place and admire it, but right now it was the people in the room who were important, and everywhere she looked were sights that made her eyes nearly start from her head.

She saw a woman dressed with perfect authenticity as a schoolgirl in a short pleated skirt, which had been pinned up to expose her voluminous flannel knickers. A naked man, on his knees and fastened on a leash like a dog, grovelled at the feet of a woman dressed in a rubber bodysuit. Another man whose cock was poking out of his unzipped trousers, openly fondled himself while maintaining an apparently unrelated conversation with the male guest beside him. And nobody appeared to be turning a hair . . .

Not knowing which way to look, and not daring to wonder what she might see next, Clover continued to track Olivia though the glittering throng, towards the focus of interest in the room, and the source of the agonised cry that had rung out a few moments ago. Olivia nodded and spoke to one or two people as they progressed, and even paused once when a man caught hold of her and kissed her hard on the mouth. As Clover observed the kiss, she saw the man's hand snake under Olivia's short skirt and from the rough, thrusting motion, it was obvious his fingers were in her sex. Olivia made a whimpering sound, and bore down for a moment, then the man released her and she skittered away from him, grinning.

Oh God, what do I do if someone tries to grope me? Clover thought frantically. It would be so easy. She had no protection at all . . .

And yet, wasn't that what she was here for? Excitement, sexual thrills, forbidden pleasure . . . And how much more forbidden and perverted could you get than having the fingers of a stranger searching and thrusting between your legs? Clover felt herself moisten at the very thought of it, the welling of her juices trickling unchecked down her inner thighs without underwear to sop them up.

At last she found herself standing beside Olivia in a group of people gathered in a circle. The centre of attention was a sturdy polished oak table, clearly a fine antique, across which was draped a naked, panting woman.

On closer inspection, a *partially* naked woman.

Clover's jaw dropped when she saw that the woman was strapped up in a harness of some kind. A heavy leather belt encircled her waist, and her hands were secured behind her with handcuffs. From the centre of the belt at the back, adjacent to the cuffs, a narrow leather strap bisected the woman's buttocks and disappeared into the groove of her sex, presumably to fasten again at the front. It looked chokingly tight, and Clover could only speculate what it was doing to the woman's clitoris.

But that wasn't the woman's only torment. As she wriggled against the table, it became obvious that her large breasts were bound too. Narrow leather thongs encircled them, digging in just as tightly as the crupper between her legs. The woman was blindfolded with a black silk scarf, and she was moaning. She wore high black heels – not unlike Clover's – and her naked buttocks were marked copiously with thin stripes of red.

'Has she been whipped?' whispered Clover to Olivia, as space was made for them in the loose circle around the prostrate woman.

'Shush,' Olivia murmured. 'You'll soon see.'

Clover looked around nervously, and found several faces looking back at her. Both women and men stared boldly at her, with open interest, lust even, but the most piercing and amused expression was on the face of a tall, distinguished looking man standing directly opposite her, leaning against the wall. He wasn't young, possibly in his late fifties, but his dark, penetrating, rather fierce features and a pronounced widow's peak in his greying hair made him attractive in a dangerous, hawk-like way. He smiled at Clover and nodded as if he knew her, then before she could glance nervously away, he spoke.

'Good evening, Miss Weatherby, and welcome to my party,' he said, his commanding voice carrying easily across the space between them. 'Forgive me for not welcoming you more personally, but the next stage of our entertainment is about to begin. I'm your host, by the way, Francis Xavier Black.'

'Er . . . g-good evening,' stuttered Clover, but her host was already otherwise occupied, whispering in the ear of a woman standing beside him, a whip-slim, dark-haired beauty, wearing a domino mask and skintight, vaguely Hispanic riding outfit.

Before Clover could ask Olivia about Francis and his companion, another figure stepped forward from the group. A man in jeans and a flowing white shirt, flexing a thin whip between his hands. His long dark hair and his solid, rather swarthy good looks identified him as Nathan, the young stud who'd been servicing Olivia and tormenting her the other day.

I bet he's going to be cruel, thought Clover with a sudden flash of insight. There was a gleeful, almost evil expression on the young man's handsome face. He looked hungry, as if he relished the task before him, and when he reached out suddenly and grasped the prone woman's bottom, his fingers dug into her flesh, his nails dragging callously at her stripes. When she groaned out loud, his smile widened and grew more lascivious.

'Can somebody gag this slut?' he said nastily, looking around the group. When his eyes lighted on Clover, he hesitated, as if assessing her, then they moved on, narrowing angrily when they settled on Olivia.

Clover too glanced at her companion, and her own eyes widened in surprise. A middle-aged man had come up behind Olivia and slid his arms around her. One hand was inside her jacket, kneading her breast, and the other had hiked up her skirt and was moving rhythmically between her legs. Olivia's eyes were slightly glazed, but she still managed to look back challengingly at Nathan.

The younger man's face turned to thunder and he slashed threateningly with the whip. He spun away from Olivia and back to his victim. 'I asked for a gag,' he cried petulantly.

'I think not,' said Francis Xavier Black from across the circle. 'We'd all prefer to hear Rosetta scream this time, wouldn't we?' Several heads nodded. 'And it's nicer for her if she's allowed to express her feelings.'

That seemed to be the last word on the matter, and with a mutinous look, Nathan turned back towards the helpless, strap-bound Rosetta.

His first blow fell heavily across the woman's left bottom cheek, but to Clover's surprise she didn't cry out. Maybe she'd decided that she wasn't going to give her tormentor the satisfaction?

For her own part, Clover felt a weird pang of lust at the sight of the woman's wriggling buttocks. What would it feel like to be hit like that? Surely it was agonising? And yet, to her horror, Clover found herself wanting to experience the sensations, to be that poor, tortured body, draped across a table and plagued by pain with a tight strap pressing hard on her clitoris. Her own crotch pulsed heavily, and she wondered whether she dare move a little way to the side, so she was obscured from the group, and attempt to touch herself.

But as she began to shift her weight, she sensed a presence immediately behind her. A second later, she felt someone press up lightly against her back and buttocks, and a second after that, a hand settled gently on her hip.

Clover's heart thudded hard. It was a man, of course. She could tell from the muscles beneath what felt like leather trousers lying close against the backs of her thighs, and from the unmistakably hard bulge of an erection that nestled into the barely clad groove of her bottom. The hand moved from her hip to her belly, and she saw a lean, strong arm clad in the long sleeve of a black cotton top, and a pale but powerful wrist encircled by a wafer thin, stainless steel watch – a Patek Philippe, if she wasn't mistaken. The man's other hand curved around her midriff, just beneath her breasts, tapered fingers not touching them, but somehow discreetly threatening to.

'Don't be scared,' whispered a voice that sounded vaguely familiar, as if she'd heard it before but just the once. It was a deep voice, and she noted a slight, but pleasing American accent, and fought to place it. When she did, pure astonishment made her try to turn around. Surely it couldn't be *him*? Her unknown caressor prevented her investigation, however, by tightening his arms and holding her closer against his body and his sturdy erection.

'Relax,' he whispered. 'You know I won't hurt you.'

Beginning to subside against him, Clover flinched sympathetically when Nathan laid another hard cut against Rosetta's defenceless bottom. Then another, and another, settling into steady, relentless beat, a fiercely aroused expression on his face.

As Clover's American friend grew bolder, cupping her breast, her mind still boggled at his possible identity. Olivia had spoken of him being in the group, but even so, Clover found it hard to believe what her instincts were telling her. A man like that had singled *her* out? Yet the voice was so distinctive. She remembered where she'd heard it now – on a morning chat show – and how she'd been astonished by the sly wit and subtlety of its owner. The man had a sharp intellect in a profession that did not require brains but sheer physical beauty.

A male supermodel shouldn't be smart, but Lukas patently was. And he was now gently fondling her nipple. Not to mention pressing the flat of his palm against her pubis.

I mustn't look! I mustn't look! Because if I do, I'll destroy the fantasy. A god-like creature like Lukas would never notice me in a thousand years, much less touch me. If I look round, I'll find out it's some complete geek with a bedroom voice that just sounds like his. If don't look, it *can* be him. It *can* be Lukas touching me – and wanting me too, if the hardness of his dick is anything to go by.

The pervasiveness of the fantasy almost made her knees go weak. She imagined the face of the man behind her, the pale sculpted features of the 'Urban Vampire', his cobalt blue eyes dark with lust and his full-lipped mouth shiny where he'd licked his lips in anticipation. He was delicately rolling her nipple between his finger and thumb now, making her want to buck her hips and wriggle, and when she looked down again she saw that his perfectly manicured nails were painted with clear polish. It had to be Lukas! Only a male model could get away with nail varnish and not seem effeminate.

A plaintive shriek distracted her for a moment, and she looked across to see the woman on the table writhing and sobbing in the throes of a particularly vicious cut. Nathan had unzipped his flies now, and was fondling his erect penis with his free hand. The sight made Clover gape for a moment, but when she glanced beyond, to the louche, lounging figure of Francis Xavier Black, she saw that the older man wasn't watching the beating of Rosetta at all, but had his eyes fixed on *her*, Clover!

He gave her a slow, amused smile, then nodded. Not to her, she realised, but to the man behind her, her dream of 'Lukas', who immediately began to unfasten the buttons of her suit.

'No! Oh no!' she hissed, as he drew apart the two panels of her jacket.

But he was implacable. And a moment later he was fondling her bare nipple, delicately tugging on it and making it harder and more erect than ever.

His fingertips were tantalisingly nimble, and as her hips beginning to waft, Clover looked frantically to left and to right, and around the circle. Most people were completely focused on Nathan and his victim, and only a couple were paying any attention to Clover's state of exposure. Most alarmingly of all, Olivia had completely disappeared and someone else had moved to take her place in the group.

She fought to stay still, but lost the battle almost immediately. Her pelvis jerked and Clover's companion leaned forward a little way and kissed the side of her neck. His lips were firm, and deliciously cool on her heated skin, but that wasn't what made her almost lose the ability to stand, and feel as if she was going to collapse in his arms.

For just an instant, she'd caught a glimpse of his perfect profile and the dazzle of his distinctive white-gold hair.

The man who was caressing her breast really *was* Lukas, the supermodel darling of millions. Oh God, she'd so hoped for this, after her conversation with Olivia, but she'd still not really believed it could happen . . .

'Are you okay, Clover?' The famous voice came softly in her ear again as his well-known hands both made free with her and supported her. 'Would you like to disappear for a while? Get some privacy?'

He knows my name, how has that happened? Is it Olivia's doing? Or maybe Francis's?

Befuddled and barely able to speak, Clover nodded.

'Come along then, girl,' Lukas murmured, laughing, 'let's go.' He released her, then took her by the shoulder and turned her around to face him.

Jesus Christ, a man like this just shouldn't be allowed to exist, thought Clover, feeling she might almost drop at his feet again. Lukas's beauty was everything it'd been in the magazine, magnified a thousand-fold by reality and proximity. His blue eyes pinned her like lasers while her own eyes tried to skitter about and take in every single fabulous thing about him in one look.

The face. The hair. The body . . . ooh, the body! Tall and slender, he had muscles in all the right places, and his black cotton top and tight black leather trousers caressed them all. The bulge of his hard-on made her mouth go dry and her crotch run like a river . . .

God help me! she thought, as he led her determinedly away from Nathan and his bleating victim, from Francis and the others, and towards a door at the far end of the long, glittering room.

When they left the throng behind them, and found themselves in a dimly lit corridor, Clover risked a swift glance at him again, just to reassure herself that she wasn't asleep and in some kind of vivid sexual dream. Lukas met her look with a strange, knowing smile and a little wink. It was as if he were both laughing at her and with her. Cursing herself for seeming like a pathetic, adoring little groupie, Clover really had no idea what to make of him. In spite of his solid presence, his commanding grip on her arm, and the fresh yet spicy scent of him, which seemed to be seeping into her head and liquefying her brain cells at an alarming rate, he was like a figure of fantasy to her, an erotic dream incarnate.

'What is it, little girl?' he asked, stopping her in her tracks and suddenly backing her up against the wall. 'Don't you know me?'

'I . . . er . . . yes, I know who you are,' she stammered, her heart almost stopping, as he whipped open the front of her jacket and suddenly bent down to kiss her breast.

His lips formed a tight suction around her nipple,

and Clover heard herself whimper like a kitten when his cool moist tongue flicked at her again and again. Through a haze of desire, she looked down, still unable to comprehend what she was seeing. His beautiful face, his shining hair, her naked breasts. Between her legs, her sex clenched hard and she almost came just from the sensations his mouth was creating.

Slumped against the wall, she hardly dare touch him for fear that he might suddenly disappear and she'd find herself being groped by some far lesser and undesirable man. But suddenly, Lukas lifted his face from her breast and gave her a puckish little grin. 'You can touch me, you know. I won't break or disappear. I'm completely real.'

All of a sudden, Clover wanted to laugh. She was still half off her head with desire and nervousness at the newness and bizarreness of her situation, but with that boyish, self-confident smile Lukas had unwittingly – or perhaps deliberately – given her the measure of him.

He *knew* he was adored, and adorable, and he loved it!

Clover met his laser eyes bravely, and smiled. For just a second, Lukas looked puzzled, but then he too grinned again, and slid one arm around her, cupping her bottom, while with the other he caressed her breast, thumbing her nipple.

'What is it, little girl?' he demanded, bending to kiss her neck, his teeth grazing her skin but not breaking it. 'What are you smiling at?'

'You, you arrogant bastard,' said Clover, not stopping to think or to be scared. He was kneading her bottom now, and she was loving it, just as she was loving what he was doing to her tit, and to her neck again, with his mouth, 'You really do think you're God's gift, don't you? You believe that because you're so famous and beautiful, every woman who sets eyes on you will fall at your feet and let you do anything you want to her.'

Lukas chuckled, low in his throat, the sensation delicious with his lips against her. 'But you let me feel you up even before you'd set eyes on me,' he countered, plucking deftly at her skirt, hiking it up, and then cradling her naked bottom cheek in his long-fingered hand. Clover gasped as the tips of those fingers delicately brushed her sex lips, but he didn't go any further than that, and the near-contact was almost agonising. Her clitoris felt as if it were swollen to twice its normal size.

'Touché, pretty boy!' she gasped, astounded at her own audacity.

Down below, his fingers crept across the skin of her inner thigh, then dipped into her slippery cleft.

At the same time, the door to the main room opened and a couple strolled down the corridor toward them. Over Lukas's shoulder, Clover could see that even though the woman was naked, and the man had his hands all over her, the two of them weren't so absorbed in their own activities that they didn't have time to observe others. In a deliberate display Lukas wrenched at Clover's skirt, dragging it right up to her waist, and ground his leather-clad crotch against her naked pubis.

Hot blood rushed through Clover's body, and for a moment she wanted to hide her face and die of shame. But then she thought, to hell with it! I'm getting it on with the most beautiful man in the world, what have I got to be ashamed of? Flexing her thighs, she jammed her pelvis back against Lukas's and gyrated hard, reaching around and grabbing at his tight, perfect, bottom with both hands as she did so. At the same time, she kissed the side of his neck messily, using her teeth and tongue and all but devouring him. He made a husky sound, halfway between a growl and a rumbling masculine purr, then he laughed softly in pleasure and approval.

'Sexy little cat,' he whispered, his fingers diving between her labia again and paddling in her juice, while his other hand roughly massaged her breast.

A second later, he found her mouth and stuck his tongue in hard and possessively. From somewhere behind him, Clover heard a voice say, 'Right on!'

Lust and exhilaration flooded through Clover. She was lost in world that not so long ago she wouldn't have believed existed, but, rocking her hips and writhing around against Lukas, she knew she'd found her place. She wanted this! She wanted everything! She wanted him! Tearing her mouth away from his, she hissed, 'What the hell are you waiting for, pin-up boy, aren't you going to fuck me? I don't care if you think you can walk on water. I want you inside me. Now!'

Lukas laughed again, a low roguish sound that made Clover's clitoris twitch in anticipation. Tilting her pelvis, she lifted one leg, hung on tight, and ground her bare sex against his fly. Splinters of sensation shot through her belly and she groaned. When his hands tightened on her buttocks, crushing her even closer, she nearly climaxed.

'My, my, what a kick-ass little girl you are, Clover,' he whispered, using his grip on her to work her ruthlessly against his erection. 'I never expected you to be such a sassy little slut.'

'Stop messing about,' gasped Clover, her vagina fluttering slowly as if calling out for the prick of the man who held her. 'Are you going to fuck me or what?'

'Fuck you, I think,' replied Lukas, his low, drawling voice sounding more American than ever. He released her bottom and let her settle on to her feet, then almost immediately he was unbuckling his belt and unzipping himself. 'We'll negotiate the "what" side of things later.'

A second later, he'd hooked Clover's thigh over his arm, stretching her wide open as he positioned himself at her entrance. Clover gasped. Good God, by the feel of things he was even bigger than the gargantuan Nathan!

'Are you sure you can take this, little girl?' he whispered in her ear, as if he'd read her momentarily fearful thought. He rubbed himself against her, teasing her lightly with his glans.

'Believe it!' she breathed back at him, working her hips, teasing right back at him. 'Bring it on, pretty boy, do your worst!'

Then she shrieked, clawed at his back, and started to climax in a heartbeat, as he pushed inside her.

Clover saw stars. He was so big, and yet her body accepted him, embraced him, clamped down on him, turning to liquid fire. It was difficult to breathe and she clung on to him, afraid she'd fall. She was impaled but the strength had been sapped out of her limbs.

Hazily, she looked into Lukas's face and found him smiling again, his blue eyes as dark as night, hugely dilated pupils revealing that he was far more affected by their joining than he was letting on.

'Does that feel good, my little Clover?' he said softly

in her ear, jerking his hips as he spoke, settling her even more deeply on his remarkable prick.

'I . . . it's all right,' she gasped, burying her face in his neck, no longer able to face him. Deep in the quick of her, she could feel another climax building, and the damned man had barely done anything yet. She suddenly felt like laughing. With Roger, it'd taken what seemed like hours of puffing and panting and striving, then usually nothing. Lukas just had to put it in her and she was going off like a firecracker!

'Just "all right"?' he protested, laughing again. With that he gripped her, sliding his hands over her hips and around her buttocks, then began to raise her up and down on him, lifting her almost clear, then jamming her down, right down on his full, hard length. Clover felt her belly bulge, as if her organs were displacing each time he thrust into her. On each in-stroke, she imagined him almost touching her heart.

Starting to come again, she wrapped her arms around his neck and clung on for dear life. For the second time, she quickened, climaxing even harder than before, unable to stop herself moaning out loud. Let him take that as his answer, and know that she thought he was considerably more than 'all right' . . .

When she was able to think at least half straight once more, she freed one of her hands, lifted it to Lukas's face and made him look at her.

What the hell was on his mind? What was happening behind those blue eyes? He was clearly aroused, but still he seemed detached somehow, as if he were observing her, as if she were a project he'd been assigned and he was monitoring her.

Maybe he is? Maybe I *am* his project? she thought

suddenly, wondering why she wasn't totally appalled by the idea. Perhaps Olivia, or even the mysterious Francis had told Lukas to find the new sexual ingénue, and give her a good seeing-to?

Well, I'm not bloody well complaining, thought Clover with an inner laugh, but I will get something out of this arrogant bastard, if it kills me.

'So, stud, what about you?' she gasped. 'Are you having a good time? Am I "all right" for you?' As she spoke, she clenched her inner muscles as hard as she could, finally glad of all the Kegel exercises she'd done, hoping to make herself capable of getting more out of Roger's uninspiring efforts.

Lukas's eyes shot wide open, and he muttered, 'Holy fuck!' Then, his chest heaving, he was suddenly in violent motion, thrusting hard again, but not in the controlled way he'd done before. His movements were ragged now, full of desperation, rising to climax. Clover pumped him again, feeling her own pleasure re-ignite.

With a broken cry, Lukas tightened his grip on her bottom cheeks, holding her down hard on his cock, as his fingers dug cruelly into her tender skin. The tiny pain triggered Clover's third climax, and as she spasmed, she laughed out loud, coming spectacularly.

This is it! she thought, feeling the inner ripple that meant Lukas was ejaculating.

This is it! I've found the secret world, and the most beautiful man on earth is coming inside me!

CHAPTER

6

I look as if I've been dragged backwards through a hedge in a hurricane, thought Clover, staring into the mirror in the bathroom. Lukas had directed her there when they'd finally uncoupled.

She poked at her hair, which was now more down than up, managing to regain some semblance of her style, and dabbed at her eyes, removing several small smears of mascara or liner that were giving her a panda look. The lip-stain, miraculously, had lived up to Olivia's prediction and was still firmly in place. Touching her fingertip to her lower lip, Clover acknowledged that her mouth was somewhat redder than it had been before, no doubt due to the savage, bruising force of Lukas's kisses. And her own . . .

'What got into you, girl?' she asked her reflection, then giggled.

She knew perfectly well what had got into her, and rather alarmingly, some of it was coming out again.

She'd mopped herself the best she could between her legs, but she could still feel the odd little trickle of Lukas's semen.

Her face wore Olivia's now familiar smug, creamy expression, that well-fucked, multi-orgasmic grin.

I've just had sex with the world's most famous and beautiful male supermodel, thought Clover, impressed with her reflection, even though she looked dishevelled and thunderstruck. How many women have been able to say that? And felt his spunk seeping down their legs?

But what now?

A man like Lukas had to be in huge demand at a party like this, and Clover was well aware that she was a newcomer, untutored, and naive in the ways of Olivia and her friends. But for all that, she wasn't a fool. Lukas had been 'assigned' to her, she was sure of it, requested to initiate the little innocent, probably by Olivia or by Francis Black. She couldn't expect a stud like Lukas to hang around now he'd done his duty, especially as, according to Olivia, straight sex was the least of his interests.

He was probably spanking some willing and more experienced woman and laughing his designer socks off at how easily he had conquered little Clover.

And yet she couldn't find it in her to feel cross or resentful. It all came back to the fact that even being with him once was a privilege, which thousands of women only dreamed of and never stood a chance of achieving in a lifetime.

I suppose I'd better show my face, she thought, frowning now, and wondering how she was going to get home and with whom. What if Olivia was still involved in some 'scene'? What if she'd gone off with a man? Or woman?

I'm here on my own now, a relative novice in a den of debauchery. What am I going to do?

Panic surged up, but almost as quickly, Clover set her jaw. Don't be a wimp! she told herself. If Olivia wasn't around, she'd grab a drink, drift around for a while, and if she still didn't show, she'd go home on her own. She had a door key in her purse, and it would be a simple matter to grab one of the ever-circulating maids to discover where that purse was. Panic over.

Taking a last look at herself in the mirror and deciding that there wasn't a lot she could do about such a disaster zone, Clover quietly opened the bathroom door and slipped outside.

Only to get the shock of her life when she found Lukas waiting for her, leaning nonchalantly against the wall opposite and staring at the ceiling.

Clover's breath caught in her throat. In that pose, with his shining blond hair, he looked like an angel. A black-clad, rather dangerous-looking one, but angelic nonetheless. Incongruously, too, he was holding a shiny blue and silver gift bag, swinging it from one finger, to and fro, rather slowly. After a split second, he lowered his gaze and gave Clover a ravishing grin.

'Hello again, Clover,' he said softly. 'I've been waiting for you.'

'Why?' said Clover, blurting out the first thing in her head. She felt her face go pink with embarrassment, as if she were one of his adoring fans. It hardly seemed possible that not too long ago, he'd been inside her. He was suddenly a celebrity again, and she was a provincial nobody. With some space between them he seemed more spectacular than ever.

Lukas wasn't the tallest man she'd ever met, perhaps just under six feet, but he certainly had the most commanding presence. His body was lean, but muscular, and his legs were amazing, long and fabulously shaped, and flattered by his leather trousers. Even though she'd just had him, Clover wanted him again.

Especially when he hit her with that grin.

'Because I thought we ought to get to know each other,' he said easily, pushing himself off the wall and taking a step towards her.

Oh God, thought Clover, her knees going weak. A part of her wanted to run, knowing her constitution couldn't take much more Lukas and still keep her upright; the other part wanted to fall down before him and give him a blow-job.

'Oh, and that would be other than in the biblical sense,' she answered pertly, amazed at her own boldness, given that insane messages were whizzing around her nervous system and that her brain seemed to have short-circuited.

Lukas chuckled, and stepped even closer, making Clover fight to stop herself retreating. 'Here, I've got a present for you,' he said, handing her the bag. 'I thought you might need them.'

Puzzled, Clover peeped inside, then delved in amongst the crumpled blue tissue paper and brought out the bag's contents.

A pair of lace panties. Not hers – in fact far more modest and decorous than her g-string – but still red, extremely pretty, and very expensive looking. They were made of silk and felt like cobwebs between her fingers.

'Thank you,' she muttered, wondering where Lukas had conjured the garment from, and how he'd managed to find skivvies just her size.

'Well, aren't you going to put them on?' he said, reaching out and taking the gift bag from her, then tossing it on to a mahogany side table that stood close by.

Clover glanced behind her at the bathroom door, but when she looked back at Lukas, he was regarding her mockingly. How insane was it to want to scuttle into hiding to put on a pair of knickers when they'd just had the hottest sex together in plain sight of people passing down the corridor.

'Of course,' she said, flashing him a confident smile. Unfurling the pretty garment, she lifted one foot and began to step into it, then felt girlishly grateful to Lukas when she swayed on her high heels and he darted forward to throw a supporting arm around her waist.

'Th-thank you,' she stuttered, when the pants were up and her skirt was down, and the sudden sense of safety, of being covered again made her feel almost tearful.

'Come on, sweet Clover, let's get a drink,' said Lukas, dropping a kiss on the top of her head, then guiding her along the corridor, his arm still firmly wrapped around her waist.

When they returned to the upstairs reception room where they'd observed Rosetta being beaten by Nathan, the party seemed to have thinned out somewhat. There were still a few groups of people standing around chatting, and some even watching a couple slowly fucking on the polished oak table, but the atmosphere low-key and there was more space and places to sit. Lukas guided Clover to a couple of leather armchairs in a corner, and once they were settled, facing each other, he signalled to a passing maid, then murmured in her ear.

As the maid scuttled away, Lukas leaned back in his chair, crossed his long legs, and linked his hands behind his head. 'So, Clover, what do you think of your first London fetish party?' he said, his tone soft and casual, yet loaded with challenge.

Dear God, what did she think of it? Her head was too crammed with impressions to be able to voice, or even pinpoint just one of them. She was in overload, and having trouble processing even the fact of sitting there with Lukas.

The leather of the armchair was fragrant and luxurious, and its surface blessedly cool through the sheer nylon of her stockings. But deep in her belly, a hot core of desire still burned, despite all the orgasms she'd had while fucking Lukas. Something in her craved more, a chance to sample the type of treatment Rosetta had experienced . . . But in her heart and gut she knew that wouldn't happen yet.

'It's different,' she said airily, trying to seem calm and unaffected in the face of Lukas's burning blue stare. 'Are they all like this?'

'Pretty much. Sometimes they're smaller and you know everybody. But generally they're very much like this.' He glanced around the room, then flicked his gaze back to her. Very intently. 'You know, sometimes, I might not be as nice to you, Clover. There might be times when lovemaking isn't what I want. Do you think you can handle that?'

Clover's heart gave a heavy thud. It was as if he'd

read her mind and detected her yearning for something darker and more twisted than the thrilling but straight sex they'd shared. She imagined him beating her with a switch, the way Nathan had beaten that woman, but even as her mind threw up the picture, it also latched on to something he'd just said. A form of words that seemed incongruous, but which made her quiver almost as much as the thought of being punished.

'Was that what just happened? What we did? Was it lovemaking?' she said, challenging him as boldly as she dared.

Lukas laughed, a soft, sexy, honest sound that made her want that, or any other form of lovemaking, all over again.

'Well, it was for me,' he said, uncrossing his long legs, as the maid approached them with two tall, frosty glasses on a tray. 'Wasn't it for you?'

Clover thought about the question, but only needed a couple of seconds. Yes, he was right, astoundingly enough . . . Yes! She'd felt closer to Lukas slammed up against the wall in that corridor than she'd ever felt with Roger in bed. She didn't know Lukas at all, but their connection had been more than physical, no matter how animal the sex.

'Yes,' she said thoughtfully. 'Yes, I'd say it was, as crazy as that sounds.'

'Well, there you are then,' he answered roundly. The maid discreetly placed a glass beside each of them, on the antique side tables adjacent to their chairs. Although the young woman's composure was faultless, and she kept her eyes respectfully lowered, it was obvious that she was just as dazzled by Lukas's beauty as Clover was. When he gestured for her to stay, a telltale blush crept up from the prim white collar of her uniform.

Lukas lifted his glass and tilted his glass towards Clover. 'To lovemaking,' he said, 'in all its forms.' He took a sip of water, his throat undulating sexily as he swallowed.

'In all its forms,' murmured Clover, drinking too, and thinking how glad she was that he'd chosen water and not yet another glass of champagne. It was worrying too, though. How could a man she'd known for little more than an hour so perfectly read her mind?

Lukas drank some more water, all the time watching Clover, then put his glass aside again. His gaze seemed to burn her, to challenge her somehow. *What's he up to?* she wondered, realising that something was afoot, but not knowing quite what. She glanced at the maid, who was still standing obediently beside them and trying to look at the polished toes of her old-fashioned buttoned shoes but failing miserably in the face of Lukas's irresistible allure.

Clover's eyes flicked between Lukas and the confused young woman, and suddenly she understood. A lesson was at hand, a piece of education, but she wasn't sure whether it was for her benefit, the maid's, or even simply Lukas's.

Whichever it was, the waiting was over. Lukas gave the maid a cool, unsmiling look, then nodded slowly. 'Prepare yourself,' he said quietly, his voice not cross or even stern, just perfectly level and neutral.

The maid visibly trembled, and the sight of her reaction made Clover shake too, and feel the need to draw in a great breath.

Oh God, it's going to happen. He's going to do it.

Biting her lips, the maid set aside her tray and began

to fumble with her skirts, hauling them upwards and revealing a wealth of white petticoats beneath the full black skirt. Dropping the hem twice, she finally managed to get the whole mass up into a bunch at her waist, exposing her knickers, which were the full, archaic bloomer style, and the tops of her stockings, which were held up with thick elastic garters. The poor girl looked as if she was about to cry, or maybe have an orgasm, or both.

She's besotted with him, thought Clover, as the young maid just stared, frozen, at Lukas, as if he were some kind of god. Maybe he was, to her.

'Please proceed,' he said, still without a trace of impatience and barely even emotion. Clover found it hard to equate his dispassionate, almost robotic demeanour with the frantic, deliciously frenzied man who'd fucked her to a standstill in the corridor. And yet they were the same, and she knew that even while they'd been jerking and thrusting against each other against that wall, there'd been a core of stillness inside Lukas. Just as there was a hidden heart of passion burning inside him right now.

This is a message to me, isn't it? Clover thought. He's telling me that he and I might be involved at some time in the future, but that it won't always be about me, or even *with* me. Third parties may be involved, one or more people . . . One on one is rare in this scene, it's too straight, too conventional.

The nervous young maid was pulling down her voluminous knickers now, but Lukas's eyes were watching Clover's face, not the embarrassed girl. Clover gave him a long, steady look, trying to tell him that she understood the situation, that she was up for it. Not a flicker of reaction disturbed the sculpted perfection of his features, but the very faintest of nods told her the message was received and understood.

Finally, Lukas glanced at his intended victim, his blue eyes flicking from her face to her sandy-haired crotch and back again. His impassivity seemed to suggest that she didn't excite him, that her groin was of little or no interest to him, yet when Clover glanced at *his* groin, she could see a distinct bulge forming behind the leather at his fly.

Again, not about me, she thought, then realised that maybe she was involved in the process after all. Perhaps it was the silent dialogue between them that was making him hard, not the maid exposing herself, or the prospect of punishing her.

'Turn around,' Lukas instructed quietly, and the maid obeyed him, shuffling her feet and moving awkwardly in an effort to keep her knickers around her knees and stop them from slipping down.

The girl's bottom was quite plump and very pale, obviously untouched. Clover gasped when Lukas leaned forward in his seat and began to touch the girl's unmarked skin. His tapered fingers glided over the rounded flesh, tracing the underhang and the upper thighs, then floating inwards towards the darker, forbidden groove. Without warning, he pressed a fingertip against the girl's anus and involuntarily she yelped and jerked away from him.

'Be still!'

For the first time there was a hint of the dominant in Lukas's voice. He still spoke in a low tone, but beneath the even, minimal words, Clover could hear steel. The young maid heard it too, and she froze, an expression of terror and adoration on her face.

'Bend over. Then part your legs and hold yourself open,' Lukas continued, and even though she whimpered softly, the girl sprang to obedience. Dipping down, she reached around behind herself and pulled apart her buttocks, holding herself wide open so that her anus was obscenely prominent.

A heavy sheen of moisture shone on the little maid's exposed sex, and feeling her own belly clench, Clover realised that she was just as wet. If only it could be her bent over like that, showing everything she'd got to Lukas. In magisterial mode, he was ten times as sexy as he'd seemed when he'd been inside her. She wanted him to demean her, make her exhibit herself, and to stick his fingers inside her orifices and violate her. She bit her lip, and tried to stay still and not wriggle, as he returned his attention to her, watching her face and ignoring the plight of the young maid and her position of shame.

'How would you feel if this were you, Clover?' he said, his voice like black velvet, his eyes like blue stars.

'I . . . I'd feel turned on,' Clover stammered. 'And I'd want you to touch me.'

Lukas nodded. Had she passed some obscure test? Was that the answer he'd wanted?

'But what if I didn't choose to touch you? What if I made you pose like this, then left you, perhaps at a party, like tonight? How would you feel if you had to stand like this, showing your asshole and your snatch, and making yourself available to anyone who passed by, anyone who wanted to feel you up, or abuse you . . . or maybe put things inside you?' Revealing his own fires, he suddenly licked his lips as if the prospect of her abasement was turning him on even more, making his

84

cock harder and harder inside his tight leather jeans. 'Could you deal with that?' he asked, forcing her to hold his gaze, his own eyes steady and unblinking.

The crude words and even cruder images made Clover feel breathless. Could she? She looked at the little maid. How was *she* feeling, standing there, bent over like some living doll for Lukas's amusement? Clover couldn't see the girl's face, but she could sense her excitement. The girl was loving it! Getting off on exposing herself in the most abject way and behaving like a worshipping slave.

'Yes, I could deal with that,' Clover said slowly, feeling the low, heavy twist of desire in her belly and the twitch in her swollen clitoris. Yes, she could deal with it . . . Good God, she was longing for it! 'It's like I said in the corridor, glamour-boy,' she stared back at Lukas, challenging him boldly and getting the biggest kick she'd ever had in her life from it, 'I can take anything you can throw at me, so bring it on!'

'What do you think they're talking about?' panted Olivia, trying to keep her eyes on the huge television screen despite an enormous degree of distraction. She was sitting with Francis in a small, private viewing room. Only a very select few at the party were aware of its existence.

Three figures were visible on the CCTV: Clover and Lukas sitting opposite each other, and a maid standing to one side, showing her naked bottom.

'We can turn on the directional mike if you like,' said Francis amiably, taking a sip of his drink. Olivia knew her host wasn't a great drinker, but, as with his cigarettes, he liked to indulge himself now and again, while enjoying some sexual entertainment. In his glass was a modest measure of fine Scotch whisky and he was dividing his attention between the monitor and the activity in the room where they were sitting.

'No ... no, it's all right. I think I can more or less work it out.'

Olivia was fighting for breath, and had quite enough sensual input for the moment, thank you very much. She was about to explode into orgasm, and was fighting desperately to hold it off. A short while ago, she and Circe had shared a wager on the turn of a card and she'd lost to the beautiful brunette, one of her greatest friends and business rivals. Now they were involved in an even more critical test. Of wills, this time, and sexual endurance.

If Circe could make Olivia come in the next ten minutes, she would have dominion over her, and be her sexual 'top' for the next two weeks. If Olivia held out, and Circe failed, Olivia would be dominant instead.

Trying to focus on the screen, and the intense battle of nerves that was clearly being enacted between Clover and Lukas, Olivia found herself unable to stop groaning aloud. She was going to crash and burn here any minute, and do it big time. Circe was giving her some of the most exquisite head she'd ever had in her life, and she was critically close to orgasm. It was only pride that was making her fight the waves of pleasure that her friend's nimble, diabolical tongue was giving her. Being controlled and punished by the beautiful dark-haired woman was something that, in truth, Olivia longed for and relished.

'Your Clover shows a great deal of promise,' observed Francis, swirling the ice cubes in his glass and glancing momentarily away from the screen and towards Olivia's lap where Circe's head was bobbing determinedly. 'A lot of untutored young women would have run screaming from some of the things you've already exposed her to . . . And yet, so far, she seems to be taking it all in her stride. Enjoying it, I'd say.' He paused, smiling, as Circe brought her fingers into play, as well as her tongue, and Olivia was forced to whimper at the unexpected intrusion. 'Don't you think it would be rather delicious to give her a real test of her mettle? A proper trial?'

Olivia nodded, feeling as if she might hyperventilate any second, the stimulation was so intense. On the screen, Clover was watching closely as Lukas did something rude and bad between the maid's stretched open buttocks, and between Olivia's own buttocks a slender finger was slowly intruding. She made an uncouth sound in her throat, as Circe tightly enclosed her clitoris between her lips, then waggled her embedded fingertip in time to a heavy, fluctuating suction.

'Olivia?' prompted Francis, an impish smile on his darkly saturnine face. He always looked so much younger when he was having fun like this.

'Yes. Yes. A proper trial,' she forced out through gritted teeth. She wasn't afraid of Circe getting a chance to dominate her, but she just hated to let the arrogant bitch win!

'Do you think you could arrange it? Come up with some kind of subterfuge that would bring her completely under our influence?' Francis went on, ignoring Lukas and Clover on the screen now, even though things looked to be getting very interesting. The maid was across Lukas's lap now, and Clover's face was a picture of fascination and naked lust.

Focus, focus, focus! Olivia told herself, trying to cut the connection between her crotch, her anus and her higher faculties.

'It might not even need subterfuge,' she said, concentrating on her unexpectedly precocious young houseguest and not on what was happening between her legs. 'She might come to us of her own accord ... oh! Oh God!'

Against her will, Olivia caught her breath as a breaking wave of sensation swept through her. Her clitoris leapt beneath Circe's stabbing tongue and the inner muscles of her quim and rectum clamped down hard on the finger lodged inside her. She came like a train and lost the bet as she cried out, wailing loudly.

When her eyes finally flickered open again, she found Francis watching her calmly, and Circe lounging in another of the large, comfortable chairs that were clustered around the screen. The beautiful brunette was smirking and looked extraordinarily pleased with herself, as she put one of Francis's thin black cheroots to crimson lips that were slick with Olivia's juices.

'Do you really think so?' asked Francis, continuing the conversation as if nothing untoward had happened. 'Perhaps it might be best to come up with a little something, just to be on the safe side.'

'As you wish,' murmured Olivia, tugging down her skirt to cover her betraying loins.

'And who will be her tutor? Her first master?' chimed in Circe, the lilt in her lightly accented voice declaring her excitement and her exultation at her victory. 'Is it time to allow young Nathan a crack of the whip, so to speak?'

'No!' Olivia felt a rush of alarm, as the eyes of both

her companions pinned her to the chair.

'What's wrong?' said Circe silkily, 'You're not trying to keep him all to yourself, are you? That's very uncharitable of you, Ollie. You know that we always share our treasures.'

'It's not that. It's just that I don't think he's ready. He's too wilful. He's not schooled himself yet. He shouldn't be let loose on a novice for a long time.'

Circe looked as if she might pout, then nodded as if seeing the sense of it.

'I agree,' said Francis, the quiet authority in his voice making Olivia almost sag with relief. 'Nathan is undisciplined and greedy, and knows nothing, despite having convinced himself he knows everything. I believe that he too would benefit from a session of schooling. A long, severe regime. He has a lot more to learn about humility before he can ever be a master. Perhaps you two ladies could come up with a suitable programme? After all, you will be in each other's company quite a bit for the next couple of weeks.'

Don't remind me, thought Olivia, taking in Circe's catlike and self-satisfied expression and the fact that the dark woman had begun to openly masturbate.

'Well, I'd be glad to,' she said, schooling her voice carefully, even though her body was already rousing again at the thought of the many delights that lay ahead. A duel of wills with Circe, the initiation of pretty, talented Clover, and the well-deserved subjugation of Nathan, her uppity young stud.

'But what about Clover?' she said, turning to the screen again, and experiencing a renewed pang of desire at the sight of the rapt, open-mouthed expression on her protégée's pretty face.

'Oh, I think we can leave her in the safe hands she's already fallen into, don't you? I'm sure that if offered adequate compensation, he'll be able to tear himself away from the catwalks and the studios for long enough to assist us.'

Oh, I'm sure he will, thought Olivia, staring at the pure, solemn, angelic expression on the face of the supermodel as his hand fell with metronomic precision across the bottom of the struggling, bouncing maid.

All of a sudden, she felt extraordinarily jealous of her naive but lucky young houseguest.

CHAPTER

7

'So what do you think of Lukas?'

They'd been sitting in sleepy silence, as the car glided through the early hours streets of London, but when Olivia spoke, Clover became instantly awake. There'd been something loaded and knowing in the older woman's voice that suggested she knew a lot more about Clover's activities during the evening than she ought to have done . . .

'What do you think I think of him?' Clover challenged, still imagining she could feel the supermodel's impressive prick inside her, and see his unnaturally blue eyes threatening her with a fate far worse than that of the little maid he'd spanked for her benefit. 'He's bloody gorgeous,' she went on, aware that Olivia too was fully awake now, and watching her closely, 'I think he's amazing. The most beautiful man I've ever seen.'

'Yes, of course, I know that,' said Olivia impatiently, twitching at her skirt as if she were excited. Again.

Clover had no way of knowing what the older woman had been up to after they'd split up at the party, but there was no doubt that her friend had got her rocks off, and Clover couldn't help but wonder how.

'But did you get on with him okay?' persisted Olivia, her voice very intent. 'Did you like him as a person as well as a body?'

It was a curious question, but Clover had no doubt about her answer.

'Yes. Yes, I did,' she said, remembering the humour and self-awareness of the blond American. He was vain and arrogant, but she'd sensed a part of him that was happy to laugh at his own fame and foibles. Somewhere under that dazzling façade there was humility and kindliness.

He'd certainly been quite sweet to the poor, befuddled maid whom he'd spanked. When Olivia had appeared to collect Clover, Lukas had very gently set his victim on her feet again, helped her organise her voluminous skirts and pull up her knickers, then sent her on her way with a quiet word of praise and a kiss on her blushing cheek. If the girl hadn't been completely besotted with him before that little performance, she certainly worshipped him now.

He's the sort of man I could have a real relationship with, thought Clover wistfully. Fetishes and beatings notwithstanding, I could still like him as a friend and a lover. God, it was such a bitch that he was so famous, so gorgeous, and could have any woman in the world at the drop of his skintight leather trousers. In all likelihood, she'd probably never see him again. After all, with a schedule like his, it was unlikely that he'd attend such parties all that regularly.

Clover cast a suspicious glance at Olivia. She'd suspected something earlier, but now she was sure . . .

'Was it a set-up? Me meeting Lukas? Did you or your friend Francis ask him to look out for me?'

Olivia laughed. 'Guilty as charged. I phoned him and asked him if he'd be there after I saw the way you looked at his photographs in that magazine. I thought it would be a nice treat for you, a welcome gift to our circle.' She reached out and touched Clover's hand. 'Everyone who attends these parties is vetted. Strange as it seems, they're all good people. But not everyone is as beautiful and spectacular as Lukas, and if you'd accidentally hooked up with someone who didn't appeal to you physically, it might have put you off the whole idea from the outset.'

Clover's spirits sagged a little. 'So it was a put-up job,' she said, closing her eyes and remembering the feel of her back being hammered against the corridor wall as Lukas thrust into her. 'He was just being kind.'

'It didn't look like kindness from what I could see,' said Olivia archly. 'I'd say his heart was really in his work tonight.'

Clover shot up in her seat. What had Olivia seen? She had disappeared from the circle long before Lukas had first started touching her.

'What do you mean?'

'Uh-oh, I'm not supposed to tell newcomers about it.' Olivia bit her lip, then grinned.

'About what?'

'Francis is very much a voyeur. He has CCTV in all his homes. He says that you never know when or where something decadent will happen. All the time you're in his house, you're part of the show.'

The corridor. There'd been a camera in the corridor. That passing couple weren't the only ones to observe her being shafted by Lukas.

A surge of renewed lust washed through Clover, stiffening her nipples and making her clitoris swell and ache. I must be a raging exhibitionist, she thought, longing to touch herself right there and then, with Olivia, and probably the watchful Damian looking on. The idea of her breasts and thighs and crotch being on show while Lukas's prick surged inside her, of hidden watchers seeing her face contort as she climaxed made her burn with a fiery need for it to happen again.

The two women fell silent for a while. Clover let her mind range hungrily over the evening just passed, leaping from thoughts of sex with Lukas, to him spanking the young maid, to exhibitionism and every possible kind of rudeness. From time to time, she glanced at Olivia and found the older woman watching her, a dreamy, speculative expression upon her face.

'So when's the next party? When does it all happen again?' Clover said at last, just as the car drew up around the back of Olivia's building, in the shadowed mews.

'I don't know,' said Olivia, smiling obliquely over her shoulder as she stepped from the car on to the cobbles. 'But don't worry, my sweet, it'll happen soon. You can count on it.'

William Lucas Van Buren – now almost exclusively known as Lukas – turned off the water, stepped from his shower cubicle and reached for a thick, fluffy bath sheet. It was already well into the small hours of the morning, but he was still feeling wired from Francis's party and he knew he wouldn't sleep for quite a while yet.

He'd enjoyed himself, as he always did at such gatherings, and the thought of what people in the business – photographers, designers, magazine editors – would say if they knew where his deepest interests lay, made him smile. Even though he affected a dangerous persona on the catwalk and in photo shoots, he knew his angelic hair and perfect looks made people believe he was a good boy. God, how his real and very murky psychology would shock them. They'd have a fit if they knew their golden, glowing boy got his kicks from mind-fucking and games of sadomasochism . . .

As he towelled himself Lukas thought back to the events of Francis's gathering. He'd not been too sure about the request to provide a 'welcoming party' for Olivia's new protégée, but in Clover he'd received a pleasant and deliciously unexpected surprise. She was obviously a natural. A woman who could be submissive, when the situation demanded it, yet she had deeper fires within her, burning with power. It was all unschooled as yet, and unchannelled, but it was there all right.

Flinging the towel across the rail, he reached down and touched his cock, not really masturbating but simply assessing its lightly thickened condition. When he'd plunged into Clover's pussy, she'd felt gloriously tight, and even tighter when she'd clamped down on him, massaging him with her powerful inner muscles. That knowingness, and that spectacular ability to milk him, had almost made him come long before he'd intended to. It was only years of practice that had allowed him to contain himself, hold on and savour the moment.

And she was feisty too.

Semi-erect, he walked naked from the bathroom and out into the long, open living area of the loft he occupied whenever he spent time in London. He was aware of the fact that, from similar domiciles nearby, he was clearly visible in the softly-lit room without the curtains drawn, but the thought of watching eyes only made his penis rouse yet more. His very existence was predicated by exhibitionism, and he enjoyed his own body in its naked state just as much as others enjoyed seeing it.

You're a vain fuck, Lukas, he told himself, walking to the long modern sideboard where a tray of drinks stood, his prick swaying as he moved. Clover admired him, he knew that, but she was postmodern enough to get beyond her own basic instincts and laugh at herself, and him, for it.

'Pretty boy,' she'd called him, challenging him to do his worst, then attempting to wring him dry as he did so.

And I bet you can take it, girl, he thought, imagining some of the things he might do to her that could qualify as his 'worst'. How he'd wanted to take her over his knee instead of Polly, the sweet little maid who'd cooperated so obligingly with his tutorial. Polly was an old hand, for all her cleverly submissive act, but Clover was completely untried by hand or implement. Her reactions would be pristine, totally honest, as fresh and thrilling as the experience of a very first fuck.

Lukas poured himself a couple of fingers of Stolly, his first drink of the night. He never took alcohol at Francis's parties. He liked to be completely in control of himself, his senses sharp and clear as winter air.

He took a sip of the tingling balsamic spirit and savoured its cold fire on his tongue. While the vodka still buzzed his brain, he set the glass down on a low metal table beside the sofa, dropped to the floor and did a series of press-ups. He worked himself hard, but he didn't break a sweat, and simply enjoyed the way his penis knocked and brushed against the soft fur rug as his body rose and fell. When he leapt up again, he was fully hard, and ready to pleasure himself.

Taking another mouthful of vodka, he sank down on to the large, squashy sofa, enjoying the textured surface of the upholstery against the backs of his legs and his ass. With thighs widely parted, he took himself in hand and began to masturbate, slowly and at his leisure. As he let the velvety skin slide exquisitely over the bone-hard core within, he opened his mind and let the images pour in.

He saw Clover stripped naked and bent across the back of a chair, her bottom and her sex completely available to him. Her hands were bound together behind her, she was blindfolded and her pretty, sassy mouth was stoppered with a rubber ball-gag fastened in place with leather straps.

What to do first? How to enjoy her? Violate her? Lukas moaned softly, relishing the sensations this vision of vulnerability engendered in his cock.

He imagined striking her once, then twice, across her sweet, rounded ass with a riding whip, and then, while she was still writhing and thrashing and making uncouth gobbling sounds behind her gag, the pain burning furiously, he'd plunge himself deep into her vagina in one ruthless thrust. She'd come straight away, of course, hugely turned on by the fire in her flesh, and the fierce contractions of her channel would caress his dick.

'Oh, Clover, Clover,' he murmured absently, working himself in long, luxuriant strokes. He could feel his balls tensing, and his essence rising, but just as he relished the familiar, about-to-capsize sensation of imminent orgasm, the phone on the table beside his drink began to shrill.

'Fuck it!' he cried, but just as much a slave to the phone as anyone in the fashion business, he reached out and pressed the button for hands-free operation, then returned his fist to its cradling position around his cock.

'Lukas, my darling, I hope I haven't caught you at a compromising moment,' said a familiar, laughing voice.

Lukas recognised Circe's light accent immediately. What did that dark witch want at this time of the morning? he wondered. Circe never called to make small talk, that was for sure.

'It's all right, Circe, I'm alone. Why are you calling?' he replied, beginning to masturbate again. The exotic brunette wasn't his favourite in Francis's group – she was too blatant, often too abrasive, and an inveterate trouble-stirrer – but she had a fabulous body and knew how to wield a whip. For a moment, he imagined her, standing over him, crop in hand, then lashing him mercilessly across his bare ass, and between his fingers his dick gave a hungry leap.

'Alone? The most beautiful man in all the world? I find that hard to believe. What happened to your little ingénue tonight? I thought you would have at least lured her back to your pad so you could have her again and again . . . She seemed besotted enough.'

'I made an impression, sure,' Lukas said, keeping his

voice nonchalant despite his excited state, 'but I'm sure you know full well that Clover left with Olivia. How could she be with me when she already went home?'

Circe chuckled, a sound that seemed to dance along the length of his shaft, even though she was already halfway to annoying him.

'So it's self-abuse then, is it, *querido*? Do you have your beautiful penis in your hand, even as we speak?'

Goddamned woman! Did she have some kind of remote vision?

'What do you want, Circe? This can hardly be a social call at this time of the morning.'

'Is it hard? Are you aching to come, my sweet? I wish I was there, so I could suck that delicious swollen knob of yours.'

'Circe! Get to the point!' growled Lukas, far more affected by her than he wanted her to know. He could still remember the last time she'd felated him. It'd been after one of his occasional sessions as a submissive. He'd been hanging naked in chains, his thighs and buttocks freshly thrashed, and she'd sunk to the floor, still in her leather goddess regalia, and milked the spunk out of him with her glossy crimson lips. After that, she'd set about him with her cane again. He hadn't been able to work for a fortnight, until all the marks had healed.

'I just wanted to tell you that there's some fun ahead – for both of us. And it's about your little Clover. Francis wants to initiate her into the group and he'd like you to do the honours, seeing as she's half in love with you already.'

Oh yeah, thought Lukas, his fingers sliding, sliding . . . It was what he'd been hoping for, and looking forward to, he realised. The formal initiation of his sweet little Clover into their circle.

'Lukas, leave your dick alone! Did you hear what I said?'

'Of course,' he said, as neutrally as he could, but well aware that Circe probably knew she was right about what he was doing. It was the law of averages. Within Francis's debauched group of perverts and libertines, libidos ran so high that frequent masturbation was the norm, a way of life.

'But what has this to do with you?' he enquired, fearful of the cruelties to which the Hispanic beauty might subject Clover. She was always ten times more savage with women than she was with men. Rivalry, he supposed, although he'd also seen her be indescribably tender with a woman she desired.

'Oh, don't worry, you'll be the sole trainer of your little friend,' said Circe dismissively. 'But at the same time I get to put young Nathan through his paces. Francis has decided that he needs bringing down a peg, and that I'm the one to do it.' She paused, and he could almost hear her battle with herself as to whether she should tell the whole story. 'Ollie's going to help me, of course, as Nathan is so in love with her, but I'm sure it'll fall to me to really bring him into line.'

'Good,' said Lukas succinctly. He had no particular hatred for the shaggy-haired young sculptor, but the man was too wild and greedy. He had no discipline, no finesse.

'Don't you like Nathan?' There was a tease in Circe's voice. What she was really asking was whether Lukas *fancied* Nathan. Which he supposed he did, in a general sort of way. He occasionally went with men when the whim took him, but he couldn't say it would break his heart if he never got to fuck, or be fucked by Nathan Ribiero. It might be nice to punish him though, and perhaps then give him a good shafting to add insult to the injury.

'I don't dislike him. But he thinks he knows it all. I wouldn't mind being a spectator during one of your sessions, though, if that's okay with you?'

'I love an audience,' proclaimed Circe. 'Although you must return the compliment. I'd love to see young Clover under the lash. With that creamy fair skin of hers she's bound to mark beautifully.' She laughed softly. 'And I'd love to watch you fucking her too.'

'Again?' said Lukas pointedly, playing his fingertips teasingly around the flaring tip of his penis. The sensitivity there made him bare his teeth.

Circe snorted with glee. 'Okay, *querido*, I admit that I watched the tape of you performing in the corridor. And you were extraordinary! There aren't many men who can shag a woman up against a wall and still look as cool and elegant as you do, even when you're coming.'

'Well, thank you kindly. I'll consider that a compliment,' Lukas said, wishing that Circe would get off the line and allow him to abuse himself in peace. With her purring and drawling across the ether, it was difficult to concentrate on his fantasies of Clover. 'Now when exactly would this little initiation-fest take place? Some of us do have a life outside the group. I have commitments. Surely Francis knows that?'

'Are you always so grumpy when you're tossing yourself off?' Circe enquired blithely. 'You needn't worry, you know, Francis will reimburse you for any precious time away from the camera.'

'When?' demanded Lukas, switching the reel of his inner movie and imagining Circe hanging in chains, while he whipped her. Her supple limbs writhed, gleaming with sweat, as he hit her again and again across her superb, rounded bottom. He could see a trail of moisture trickling down her inner thighs from her engorged pudenda. This time she was the one he wanted to screw. To grasp her hips, his thumbs digging cruelly into her punished buttocks, while he shafted her mercilessly, or, better, penetrated her anus and sodomised her. Oh, how he'd love that! To hear her shout and grunt with helpless shame and pleasure . . .

'Around the Bank Holiday. Francis is thinking of making a week of it. Having a small house party, with your Clover and young Nathan as the featured slaves. Several days of intensive training and exhibition, all winding up with a grand debauch to celebrate Francis's birthday on the twenty-fifth.'

Circe's voice made him jump, fracturing his fantasy and nearly causing him to rub himself too hard and come then and there. He drew in a deep breath, taming his excitement. Snatching away his hands, he looked down at his prick pointing ceiling-wards in all its magnificent, rampant glory. The swollen head glistened with copious pre-come and shone round and red.

'Can you make it then? Just think how disappointed Francis would be if you missed his big party,' persisted Circe. There was still a smile in her voice somehow, as if she had a hidden camera and was observing his prick too.

'I'll have to check with my booker, I might be busy,' said Lukas tightly, wanting to touch himself again, but not wanting to reveal himself to Circe.

'Oh, but, sweetheart, you must know it'll be well worth your while. You'll enjoy working on a sweet young thing like Clover. You've already started. Think how much further you can go.'

'I'll give it some thought,' said Lukas, knowing it was a certainty. How could he turn down such a delicious prospect? Especially as he owed Francis Black so much. Without the guidance and tutelage of the older man, he would never have realised his true nature. He'd have spent his whole life chasing the wrong thrills: drugs, drink, all manner of self-destruction.

'Now was there anything else, Circe?' he enquired softly, knowing that with her there was *always* something else. 'It's the early hours of the morning and I have to get some sleep.'

Circe laughed again, her voice husky. 'You'll sleep better if you're relaxed, lover. And for that you need to come. Why be so stubborn? I know you're aroused and touching yourself. Why don't we work together and we can both have a beautiful time?'

Lukas sighed. She wasn't going to be discouraged. He might as well give in to her. It wasn't as if he didn't desire Circe, because he did. He remembered the last time they'd been together, the athleticism of her body, and her complete lack of inhibition ... He'd been almost shell-shocked after the things she'd asked him – and told him – to do.

'You win,' he said softly, reaching down to encircle his cock with cautious fingers. He was very close, and he didn't want to shoot off prematurely and perhaps gasp, revealing it to Circe.

'You glorious boy,' breathed Circe. 'God, how I wish I was there with you now and I could see your perfect

103

dick. Are you fully erect? Are you caressing yourself? I'll bet that slippery, silky juice is just pouring out of that sweet little love-eye of yours.' She gasped and Lukas imagined her red-lacquered fingertips at work on her own sex.

'Yes, I've got a massive hard-on,' he said frankly, 'and I'm playing with my knob with one hand while I hold the shaft gently with the other.'

It was true. He loved to work on himself with two hands, really make a production out of the rather basic act of masturbation.

'There's pre-come all over the place, I'm running like a river. It won't be long before I shoot an enormous load.'

It sounded hilarious, really, like something out of a cheap porno flick, but he was enjoying himself now. And he had no doubt that Circe was loving it too.

'So, what are you doing, Madame C?' he enquired, shuffling in his seat so that his butt cheeks were separated and his anus was pressing and rubbing against the patterned surface of the sofa's upholstery.

'I'm lying on my bed with my legs wide open and I'm naked,' she said in a slow, sexy voice. 'I'm stroking my clit with one hand and pinching my nipple with the other,' obviously someone else with a hands-free phone, thought Lukas, 'and I have all my favourite sex toys around me, so I can use those to get myself off, if I want to.'

'Are you wet?'

'Soaking,' replied Circe, making a low cat-like sound in her throat. What *is* she doing? thought Lukas, manipulating his glans delicately with thumb and finger, wishing that Circe were here to do the same thing with her crimson-painted lips.

'The juice is just gushing out of me,' she went on, 'I

may have to change the sheets. I'm sweating too. It feels so hot – not the weather, it's just me. I'm burning up.'

'Me too, baby,' murmured Lukas, not sure whether she could hear him, but not really caring. 'Why don't you use one of your toys,' he suggested, wishing that he'd had the foresight to gather one or two items for himself. Maybe a silk or fur glove to stroke his shaft with, or perhaps something a little more dangerous? He had a sudden, intense desire to have a butt plug inside him. A really huge one, so he could feel stuffed and stretched while he wanked himself, his sensitive prostate passively stimulated by the rubber intruder. His cock leapt in his fingers at the thought of it.

'Those toys,' he said carefully, 'what have you got?'

'Ah, naughty Lukas, you're interested in my perverted little playthings, are you?' There was a sound that might have been the chink of a chain. 'Do you play with toys too, *querido*?'

'Sometimes. But sometimes, I like my sex plain and simple, no frills.'

'How do you feel about butt plugs, sweet boy?' enquired Circe, chuckling.

Goddamn the woman, she *could* read minds! Lukas pressed hard at the base of his glans, taming the flaring urge to come that threatened to end this game prematurely. He bit down on his lower lip, breathing hard.

'You like them, don't you?' Circe persisted, 'You know you do. I remember our games. I remember stuffing that beautiful arse of yours while you were in bondage. You were sobbing, and your penis was like iron. Is it like iron now, baby, just thinking about me pushing something big and hard and horrible inside you?'

'You're the one with the toys, Circe,' Lukas muttered

through gritted teeth. 'You tell *me* what it feels like.'

'Oh, but I don't have one of those here.' Circe sounded coy, and Lukas knew she was probably lying. 'I have a nice vibrator though. Can you hear it buzzing?'

There came the clear and distinctive sound of a vibrator humming, and after a second or two, gasps and soft cooing sounds from Circe. Lukas pictured the beautiful brunette stretched out on her bed, her thighs wide to show her vivid peachy sex, a long, plastic cylinder, its rounded tip applied to her clitoris . . . Unless of course, she had it inside her?

'Describe it to me. Tell me how you use it,' Lukas said, his voice harsher and less controlled than he would have liked it to be. This was a contest and he'd already weakened far too much.

There was a long pause, filled with buzzing and little gasps and mewls. After a sharp cry, Circe came back on the line again. 'Oh, that's better,' she said, sounding smug. 'Yes, well, my little toy . . . Actually it's not so little, which is why I chose it.' There was a sound of rustling, as she adjusted position. 'I just rubbed it against my clit and it made me come very nicely. I feel more relaxed now, ready for much more fun.'

'What does it look like, this thing?'

'It's long, fat and pink and made of latex, shaped like a real cock, but not nearly as pretty as yours, my love, so don't worry. It's not a substitute, just a nice extra for when I don't have a man handy.' She gasped heavily, and Lukas could hear the sound of her panting. What was she doing? Was she pushing it inside her? Oh, God, she must be. His real, non-latex cock pulsed and thickened, and he knew he couldn't hold out much longer.

'Circe!' he prompted.

'Yes! Oh yes!' She was still having trouble breath‥.g and Lukas could picture the giant rubber monster protruding between her sex lips, stretching her almost cruelly, an obscene intrusion. She would have to be wet, so wet to get it into her, but then, hadn't she said that her pussy was soaking?

'Oh, it's so big, Lukas!' she moaned. 'Bigger than you, *querido*. But don't get upset. No man is *this* big!'

Oh, I don't know, thought Lukas absently, his brain beginning to empty of all coherent thought. Looking down at his own dick, he looked unfeasibly enormous, his knob red and slick, veins standing out all down the shaft. His balls were tight and high, ready to unload. . .

'I can just imagine pushing this beauty into your little Clover. I bet she's really tight, isn't she? I bet she'd moan and cry as this monster stretched her little quim wide open. Think how rude she'd look with this poking out of her. Rude and bad and debauched, Lukas. I'd like to shove it into her while you're tied up and unable to do anything about it. Both of you helpless; her with my nasty latex big boy pushed into her and you bound up and immobile, with your cock tethered in straps and that huge, huge butt plug you love so much jammed into your arse!'

'No! No!' cried Lukas, while every nerve end in his body screamed, 'Yes!' Fire seemed to surge through his belly and shoot out in a scalding rush of semen. His cock leapt in his fingers as white skeins of seed shot through the air.

Blind with pleasure, he heard Circe laughing jubilantly.

'Oh yes, *querido* . . . Yes!'

Her throaty shout said that she was coming too.

CHAPTER

8

The sun shone down on Clover as she strode along the street, its heat magnified by the plate glass windows of the shops she passed, and by the hot city pavements beneath her feet. Shoppers and tourists jostled her, the temperature making them less considerate of others, and she could almost taste the tempers fraying around her.

She was on an errand for Olivia, one of many her hostess seemed to be finding for her. It was almost as if the older woman was avoiding conversation and situations where Clover could ask when Francis Black's next party was.

Olivia was obviously going somewhere though. She was out every night, and often slipped away from the atelier during the day. And whenever she came back, she looked almost beatific, but very often exhausted as well. Clover could tell that Olivia was being punished wherever she went, because she frequently moved with care, and winced on sitting down when she thought nobody was looking.

Why won't she tell me about it? I thought she was going to teach me? Initiate me? Clover shifted the large portfolio beneath her arm. The smooth, faux leather surface of it was sticking to her bare, sweaty arm. In fact, the whole of her body felt bathed in perspiration, but it was the sweat of frustration more than the muggy weather.

She wanted to enter the secret world again. She wanted to learn more, try things. Goddammit, she wanted an opportunity to see Lukas again, if only to see if he actually remembered a girl he'd once screwed against a wall. But instead, here she was, trudging the streets of London, lugging this bloody portfolio around to Olivia's button designer.

Shit, there must be an easier way! thought Clover, tugging at the neckline of her light summer dress and wishing she were lying on a shady patio somewhere, preferably with the high and mighty Lukas crouched between her legs, giving her head.

Why couldn't Olivia just courier the damn designs round to the button people? Or even send the images as email attachments? And for that matter, surely she ought to see the people and the buttons herself? She was the designer, after all . . .

But no, they were to see her original sketches, pick out some samples of buttons suitable for the garments pictured, and send them back with Clover.

I should have taken a taxi, or the Tube, thought Clover, suddenly feeling overwhelmed by the sea of faces coming towards her on the pavement. But it had seemed a shame to go below ground, or be cooped up in a stuffy cab on a beautiful day like this, and the button maker's boutique was only a walk of twenty minutes or so from Olivia's premises. Clover had been once before, with Olivia, so she knew exactly where it was.

Or did she?

Glancing up at a street sign, she began to wonder if she'd missed the corner that she should have taken. It was so hot, and the frazzled crowd seemed intent on jostling her. There was a pavement café-bar to her left, and the idea of a long, cold drink was appealing. But maybe she should get her errand out of the way first. Gritting her teeth and trying to re-orientate herself, she focused on the street ahead, trying to recognise the turning.

But suddenly, her heart leapt and started thudding. Ahead, she saw a tall figure whose white-gold hair glinted in the sunlight like the helm of some heroic knight on a quest.

Was it him? But if so, what was he doing roaming around the grubby streets of London on a weekday afternoon? Shouldn't he be somewhere glamorous? A photo shoot? Or even out of the country?

Yet when she sped up her pace, and bumped into a German tourist for her trouble, getting a very stern look, she grew more and more sure that the slender male figure ahead was Lukas. She'd know that smooth, sexy strut anywhere, and he was even wearing black again, tight jeans and a loose, linen jacket. When she got closer, she could see that he looked as cool and unfazed as ever and not the slightest bit hot and bothered by wearing a dark colour on the warmest of days. Behind a pair of deeply smoked shades, his eyes were unreadable.

Clover opened her mouth to call out to him, then

immediately thought better of it. He might be pissed off if she identified him in the street. It must be difficult going about your normal business when you were so famous and eye-catching. In fact, thinking about it, Clover couldn't imagine why he was actually walking around like this and not in a taxi or an air-conditioned limousine.

And anyway, what would she say to him?

'Hi, me again . . . It was great the other night, and when are we going to get together again for some of that spanking you demonstrated?'

A hassled shopper gave Clover an odd look, and she suddenly realised she must have been muttering aloud. She glanced around her in embarrassment, and to her alarm, saw that Lukas had picked up his pace and was disappearing into the crowd. Clover speeded up too, starting to pant in the heat and feeling sweat trickling down between her breasts and into her crotch. She sprinted ahead, then skidded to a halt again when Lukas stopped, turned and smiled at a pretty oriental girl who'd just accosted him. She held up a notebook and pen and, slipping his sunglasses into his pocket, he gave the girl his autograph, his expression friendly and interested and not in the least bit impatient. He even slid his arm around the young girl's shoulders and posed while a passer-by was dragooned in to take a photograph of them together.

Clover lurked in a doorway watching. Oh, you're such a smooth bugger, she thought. What would that sweet young thing think if she found out what you're really like? She'd run a mile if she knew you were probably wondering what she'd look like face down across your knee.

When the photo was taken, and Lukas and the young Japanese girl had exchanged bows – much to her obvious delight – he glanced around him, his confident blue gaze gliding dangerously in Clover's direction. Her heart thudding, she darted back into her doorway, and pretended to look at a display of ugly, almost unwearable shoes. Had he seen her? She waited, hardly daring to breathe, but no tall, black-clad figure appeared to ask her what the hell she was doing. A few seconds later, she popped out again, and, to her horror, discovered that he'd disappeared completely.

'Shit!' she said, setting off at a half run towards the area where she'd last seen Lukas. She glanced from side to side, nearly bumping into passers-by again, but she couldn't see him, and almost felt like crying.

'Bugger! Shit! Damn! Fuck!' she chanted to herself, no longer caring what anyone around her thought.

'Hey! What's all the cussing about?' A firm and very strong hand settled on her shoulder, and before she could even turn around to confirm its owner's identity, darts of sensation shot from the point of contact straight down to her groin.

Starting to shake, she turned . . .

Lukas looked down at her, an amused expression on his perfect, sculpted face. Smug git! thought Clover, realising he must have performed the same trick. He'd dodged into a doorway and laid in wait for her. Obviously he'd seen her when he'd scoped the street a couple of minutes ago.

'So, what's the problem?' he said amiably, his cool blue gaze panning slowly from her feet to the top of her head. Clover felt herself blush even hotter. God, what would he think of her? The summer dress she was wearing was one of her own, and very simple and unsophisticated, her hair was a mess, and her face was red and probably shiny with sweat. She was wearing just the tiniest bit of make-up; mascara and lip-gloss.

Mr Perfecto! Clover thought mutinously, glancing at his long, beautiful hands and imagining them touching her. Or even smacking her ... What would that feel like? She could only imagine. She hadn't even dared to try slapping herself.

'Oh nothing. It's just such a muggy day, and this damned portfolio thing of Olivia's is so heavy and awkward to carry. I should have taken a taxi, but it seemed extravagant. It's not that far.'

'Where are you going?' Lukas flicked back his coat, and shoved his hands in his pockets. He seemed to stand so lightly on the pavement, and his body was completely relaxed, as if nothing in the world could ever bother him.

Clover explained her errand, trying to make it sound as if it were something she'd chosen to do for a change, rather than because she was nothing more than a glorified step 'n' fetchit for Olivia. Judging by Lukas's knowing smile, it was obvious he knew the score.

'Is it urgent?' he asked, 'I mean ... do you have to be there by a certain time? I thought we might go somewhere and get a cool drink. You look as if you could use one.'

Thanks, thought Clover, looking at Lukas, so cucumber cool and composed in the heat, despite his funereal clothes. The only concession to the close atmosphere was the opened buttons at the neck of his silky black shirt. She hesitated, knowing she really ought to deliver the sketches, but fatally tempted by the prospect of a drink with this enigmatic man whom she desired all the more for having had sex with him once.

'Okay, just a quick one,' she said. 'But then I've got to get these to the button place.'

'Good,' replied Lukas, his blue eyes upping a notch in brightness and intensity. 'I know a place nearby where it's quiet and cool, and we can talk.'

About what? Clover questioned silently, as he took the unwieldy portfolio from her and tucked it under his arm. With his free hand on her waist, he gently guided her along the pavement.

A short while later, Lukas had led her down a side street, and they fetched up in front of a tall anonymous building with a basement entrance. Lukas descended first then courteously handed Clover down. The black-painted door was unmarked, and she felt a deep shudder of disquiet ripple through her.

'What is this place?'

'Just a private club. Nothing to worry about,' he said with a grin, but Clover found herself more concerned than ever. At Francis's party she'd discovered what often went on behind the most innocuous façade.

And yet . . . wasn't this what she wanted? Perhaps this was just another portal to the secret world? When Lukas pressed an entry buzzer, then spoke softly into the speaker, excitement thrilled through her and displaced a lot of her qualms. She even felt a trickle of wetness between her legs.

They were admitted into a wood-panelled subterranean foyer, lit by a series of ornate lamps. There was an atmosphere reminiscent of a discreet and very exclusive gentlemen's club and Clover wondered if indeed that was what it was. Although why an American male supermodel should be a member, she couldn't really imagine. He seemed suited to some place far 'younger' and trendier.

'Good afternoon, sir, it's nice to see you again,' said a feminine voice, and Clover glanced around to see a beautifully groomed middle-aged woman, dressed in a very sober black dress, standing behind a reception desk on which lay an open ledger.

'Hello, Isabel, good to see you too,' said Lukas, effortlessly switching on the dazzle. The concierge didn't strike Clover as the type of woman to be easily impressed or swayed by anyone, but even so, she exhibited a slight, but distinct 'melt' in the face of his beauty. She even seemed to bat her eyelids as she pushed the ledger across the counter towards him.

Clover craned forward, intrigued to see what name he'd used to sign in, but to her disappointment, the single word 'Lukas' was all that he wrote. Next to it, he added 'and guest', which also seemed to be adequate for the concierge.

'Would you like to leave this here?' Lukas hefted the portfolio.

Clover felt a pang of disquiet. Weren't there supposed to be some very exclusive designs in that thing? Surely she shouldn't take her eyes off it? But then again, this was obviously a very exclusive establishment, and not just anybody could wander in off the street. It would be okay to leave the portfolio with the very efficient and watchful looking Isabel, she decided.

'Come along, Clover,' murmured Lukas, his voice low as if in respect for their hushed and hallowed surroundings. Clover wondered for a moment whether his tie-less state, and her casual summer dress and flat-ties would be smart enough for them to enter the club itself, but Isabel said nothing and they walked through the foyer towards an open double door.

The impression of a gentlemen's club became even stronger as they entered a long, softly-lit room. The furnishings were predominantly leather armchairs and Chesterfields, not unlike those in Francis Black's sumptuous home, and dotted across the room were golden pools of light from antique lamps placed on low, occasional tables. Several small groups of people were sitting, talking quietly and drinking, some in couples, others in threes or more. As Lukas led her across the room, Clover heard what sounded like a soft moan coming from the far side, but as it emanated from an area of shadow, she couldn't see what was going on.

'What is this place really?' she asked Lukas. He was taking her to the very corner of the room, to a secluded cluster of chairs in a less well-lit area.

'As I said, a private club . . . for people who share the same interests,' he said, indicating that she should sit down.

Hairs stood up on the back of Clover's neck, and where the sweat was drying in her cleavage and on her stomach and the backs of her thighs, she suddenly felt shuddery. She had no doubt what those 'same interests' were.

As Clover took her seat, a rather elderly waiter arrived to serve them, and without reference to her, Lukas ordered drinks. A mineral water for himself and a small brandy for her.

'But I don't drink brandy,' she protested, staring at him and feeling very much like a rabbit in the glare of approaching headlights. He was sitting back, utterly relaxed, in the large leather chair, his chin resting on one knuckle, his other arm draped lightly across his body.

'Oh, I think you'll enjoy it today,' he said in that neutral, tantalising voice he'd employed the other night when dealing with the pretty young maid. 'You're not wearing tights or stockings, are you?' he added, seemingly apropos of nothing that had gone before.

'No. No, I'm not.'

'Stand up again, Clover, then pull your skirt out from beneath you and sit down again. Feel how pleasant the leather is against your bare thighs.'

Clover realised immediately that the parameters of normal behaviour were far behind them now. In the short space of time it had taken to arrive here, they'd travelled to another country. They were in the secret world. Without demur, she did as she was told, and found the sleek, cool surface of the leather upholstery delicious against her suddenly heated skin. It was vaguely demeaning too. She'd been robbed of protection somehow; exposed even though she was chastely covered.

The waiter arrived with their drinks, and all the while the man was fussing with glasses and bottles and coasters, Lukas's eye remained focused on Clover. His gaze never wavered, indeed, she could swear that he never blinked once. When she shuffled against the leather, his beautiful mouth curved into a slight smile.

Oh God, what is he doing to me? thought Clover. Lukas wasn't even touching her, yet he had her every nerve end on fire. Her nipples were like stones, she had a heavy, frustrated ache in the pit of her belly, and she could feel her juices seeping thickly through her panties and anointing the leather beneath her. She didn't know precisely what she wanted – other than an orgasm – but whatever it was, she wanted it soon.

Taking a sip of the brandy, she nearly spluttered, but after a moment its smooth, rich, aromatic burn seemed to soothe her. She felt ready for whatever Lukas had in store for her.

Which began almost immediately . . .

'Take your panties off,' he said quietly, his voice impassive, although his American accent suddenly sounded particularly pronounced.

'But—'

He silenced her with his steady blue gaze, and Clover found herself reaching under her skirt and tugging at her white cotton knickers. She felt a moment of disappointment that she'd not put on something more fancy, more seductive, and yet she sensed that the plain, almost girlish underwear might find Lukas's approval.

'Hand them to me, then make sure your skirt is lifted.'

Clover complied, her hand shaking when her fingers tangled momentarily with Lukas's around the white cotton bundle. As she tweaked her skirt, then settled her unprotected quim down against the leather, he unfolded her knickers and perused their saturated gusset.

Clover felt her face burn. Not only at the blatant and no doubt odiferous evidence of her arousal, but also because she could feel a fresh rush of silky juice pouring out on to the leather beneath her. She was sticking to the surface of it, almost sealed by her own honey. If she rocked her hips slightly, she knew she could stimulate her clitoris against the chair's seat, but she knew Lukas would see her move and know exactly what she was doing.

'You're such a naughty girl, aren't you?'

He was keeping his amazing face straight, but there was laughter in his eyes, Clover knew it. Here it comes, she thought, almost laughing herself. The segue, the reason, the excuse . . .

'I think I should punish you, don't you?' He looked at her, eyes level and penetrating, challenging her to turn and run, as he slid her panties into his jacket pocket, then shrugged out of the jacket and tossed it over an adjoining chair. Still pinning her to her seat with his laser gaze, he unbuttoned the cuffs of his shirt and slowly rolled them up.

He's got strong wrists. He can really hurt you, Clover told herself while Lukas unshipped his Patek Philippe and placed it on the table beside his chair.

'So, what do you think?' prompted Lukas, slowly running his thumb over the palm of his left hand, as if testing its texture and preparedness. Unable to look him in the eye any more, Clover found her eyes skittering to his crotch. The size of the bulge she saw there made her gulp.

'Y-yes, I suppose you should,' she stammered in answer to his question.

Oh God, how much did it *really* hurt? The maid, and the other woman she'd seen punished at Francis Black's had shouted and struggled. Surely they didn't do that for no reason? What have I got myself into? she thought frantically, wondering if she dare, even at this late stage, chicken out. She had a feeling that despite everything – especially that enormous hard-on – Lukas would immediately respect her wishes.

119

Don't be a pathetic wimp! she told herself. At least try it this once. If you're going to do something pervy, you couldn't have a more thrilling partner. Just imagine all the women all over the world who must get spanked by fat, ugly, balding men, and you've got the idol of millions to do the job for you.

'Well, I can't punish you from here, can I?' he said gently, then nodded downwards, towards his lap and his strong thighs braced to take her weight.

Clover gulped again and got slowly to her feet. When she reached him, he took her by the hand and guided her face down across his legs, the action as gentle and courtly as if he were a beau, squiring a lady at a cotillion.

He must be able to feel me trembling, thought Clover. In fact she was shaking so hard, she was surprised she wasn't already slipping off his knee. But Lukas steadied her, shifting her centre of balance with his own thighs, and a second or so later, she was stable and in position.

Her body was so hot that the air in the room seemed frigid when he finally lifted the skirt of her summer dress and bared her bottom. Who else is looking? Clover wondered, then forgot about anyone in the club, or anywhere else, as Lukas's long, cool fingertips settled assessingly on her left buttock. With slow precision, he palpated the flesh as if testing its resilience, or its vulnerability to pain and injury. In spite of her fear, however, Clover found herself not flinching, but almost pushing her arse into his hand. Between her legs, her sex seemed to flutter and her clitoris swell. Just this light, disinterested touch and she was ready to come. She could smell the pungent aroma of her own arousal even over the heady scent of Lukas's exotic cologne.

'Ow!'

He hadn't asked her if she was ready, and the sudden impact of his hand – as hard as a wooden board – against her bottom cheek was an astonishing shock.

God, it hurt so much! Far more than she'd expected. And the second one hurt even more, making her kick and shout and struggle before he'd barely even begun. Why had she fooled herself that a simple smack with his hand wouldn't be much? It was terrible!

The third blow was worse . . . and the fourth worse than that. Lukas was dividing his attentions between both her bottom cheeks, and within moments both were burning arcs of pain. Clover yelled at each blow, and despised herself for it. She'd had some vague plan that if this ever happened to her, she'd be brave, and impressive, and maintain a perfect, stoical silence, but right from the first impact she'd been yowling.

Yet he didn't reprimand her for it. He just went on carefully and methodically turning her arse into a mass fiery redness. An inferno that seemed to sink through her and pool in the quick of her sex.

As the tears dripped ignominiously from the end of her nose, Clover realised with a sudden jolt that it wasn't just the pain that was making her cry, but frustration and desire too. Her sex was as swollen and irritated as she knew her buttocks must be, and her wriggling and rocking against Lukas's lap was as much to bring her clitoris into contact with some direct stimulation as it was to avoid the spanks he was raining down on her.

'P-please,' she moaned, grinding herself against his thigh and praying that he understood what she was asking for . . .

But of course he knew! That was what punishment and bondage and sado-masochism was all about, wasn't it? It was about getting to that beautiful place, but going around the most twisted and tortuous of back roads to get there. And the beautiful place was the goal of both the person who meted out the punishment *and* the one being punished . . .

'What do you want?' asked Lukas softly, his hand never missing a beat. In fact, Clover could swear he hit her harder. She squealed when he used one hand to pull apart her buttocks, then landed a particularly stinging smack straight across her anus.

'I . . . I . . . want . . . Agh!'

Another blow clean across the tender vent of her bottom. The fire of it shot straight to her clit, and it throbbed, once, almost on the point of orgasm.

'Clover?' he prompted gently, his spanking hand stilling, but the other pressing hard into the groove of her bottom, stirring the hot, red rage in her flesh.

Oh no! thought Clover, astonished. What was happening to her? He'd stopped spanking her and it was as awful as when he'd started. She felt her hips swirling and lifting, locked in a mad dance of conflicting drives. She wanted to grind her clitoris against his hard thigh and get the release her body was craving; yet she also wanted to entice her beautiful tormentor into belabouring her punished flesh even more.

'I don't know . . . I don't know what I want,' she said, snuffling through her sobs. God, she sounded so pathetic!

But I'm not pathetic, she thought, an instant later. Her backside was burning, but it was something she'd chosen – and would still choose. Some women would never have the guts to go through even a part of what she'd discovered so far; or the imagination to see what rewards could lie at the end of such an ordeal.

As if he'd heard her inner epiphany, Lukas's fingers tightened on her bottom cheek. Each one felt like a red-hot nail driving into her.

'I've changed my mind. I *do* know what I want!' she cried, schooling her voice, even though the pain of his touch was intense. 'I want to come!' she went on boldly. 'I want an orgasm, I really, really want one,' she shifted her hips restlessly to make her point, 'but if that means I have to have more spanking first, I can take it. Do it!'

Lukas laughed, a soft, amazing, erotic sound that was as arousing as anything that had gone before it. His hand curved around her bottom, gently stroking this time, although even such a feather-light touch translated itself as torment.

'Oh, I think you've taken quite enough punishment for your first session, sweetheart,' he murmured, bending low. Clover felt his breath against the side of her neck and longed for him to kiss her there. Kiss her hard, even bite her like a vampire.

But instead, he took hold of her, bodily, and turned her over on his lap. She groaned when her punished buttocks rubbed against his jeans-clad thighs, but even that pain only served to excite her more. She stared up into his amazing blue eyes, and saw a strange mix of emotions. Arousal, an unmistakable and almost mirth-provoking machismo, all wound up with a strange and almost evanescent tenderness. But the feeling that most touched her was the look of admiration on his face. She'd done well, and he respected her for it. Lying bare-arsed on his knee, she felt his equal.

'And now your reward for being so brave,' he went on, and Clover nearly let out a giggle because when analysed, his words and the scenario they were a part of were completely absurd.

But she didn't laugh when he slid one long, slender-fingered hand between her legs, and unerringly found her clitoris. The pad of his fingertip settled on it as lightly as a hovering hummingbird and began to rotate the tiny structure in a delicate yet complicated rhythm.

Clover cried out and kicked and wriggled again, but this time not in pain. Only seconds into the exquisite digital dance, she was coming furiously, with a feeling that all heaven and earth were falling through her loins while her head was filling up with stars.

She might have called Lukas's name, but she wasn't sure of it. She only knew that her sex convulsed, again and again, and her lover continued his poetic ministrations until exactly the instant she knew that she'd really had enough.

Clover wasn't sure how long she lay across Lukas's lap, her chest heaving with the exertion of such an enormous orgasm, and her bottom still throbbing like an engine with the glowing heat of the spanking. Slowly, however, she settled back into herself, and became aware of her surroundings and the presence of the man holding her.

She didn't care one bit about the club and its patrons; her only concern was Lukas, and in particular the iron-hard erection she could feel pressing insistently against her flank.

'What about you?' she murmured, stirring across his lap and rubbing herself against the delicious, tempting bulge. She was rewarded by a satisfying gasp and a gleaming smile from his full, sensuous lips.

'Oh, I have something in mind,' he answered, his smile broadening as he lifted the very fingertip that had just pleasured her so efficiently and laid it delicately against her own mouth. 'These lips have cried long enough, Clover, my sweet,' he said, circling his finger around her parted lips and allowing her to taste the pungent, raunchy flavour of her own sex. 'It's time now to put them to another use altogether . . . Do you know what that might be?'

Clover *did* know, and with a grin, she drew his finger into her mouth to show him just how well she understood.

CHAPTER

9
_____

Lukas laughed.

'Oh, Clover, you're such a naughty little girl. I ought to spank you again for that.'

But he didn't remove his finger from her mouth, and Clover sucked on it even harder, swirling her tongue around to demonstrate she knew what she was doing.

Not that she was all that experienced, she thought, as Lukas's eyes closed momentarily in anticipation. He had the longest lashes she'd ever seen. Roger hadn't been keen on what he'd called the 'kinky stuff', which had included such universally beloved pleasures as oral sex. God knows what he'd think of spanking, she reflected.

Lukas slowly withdrew his forefinger from between her lips, then slid his arm around her shoulders and urged her off his lap and on to her knees.

Her former fiancé would probably have had an apoplexy if she'd suggested a spot of S and M. Maybe she should have done just that? Asked for some variations, then dumped him when he went all prim on her? That way, *she'd* have been the one to call off the engagement and she wouldn't have lost face.

Oh fuck! Who cares about Roger now, she thought, moving into position and gazing into Lukas's glorious face and crotch. Repressed, tight-arsed Roger was part of her past, and *this* was her future.

With a slow, almost feline grin, Lukas lounged back in the chair and linked his hands behind his head.

So that's the way it is, Clover thought. Yours truly has to do all the work, be the punished slave pandering to her master's every sexual whim.

Well, it was no hardship. She reached eagerly for the silver buckle of his thick leather belt.

With a deftness born of a longing to finally see what lay behind it, Clover tackled the belt, then the jeans' button and zip with speedy efficiency, despite the way the black-denim fabric was pushed taut by the prodigious bulge beneath it. Just how big was Lukas? In the corridor at the fetish party, they'd leapt together so quickly and passionately that she hadn't had a chance to have a good look at him. But he'd felt enormous inside her and stretched her so much her eyes had almost watered.

'Oh my God!' she whispered when she parted his fly and the monster within sprang out at her.

He was huge. Beautiful and elegantly shaped – but huge. Her jaw had dropped when she'd seen Nathan's equipment that afternoon in Olivia's workroom, but Lukas's endowments easily surpassed that of the wild young sculptor.

How in heaven's name am I going to get my mouth

round all that? Clover thought, eyeing the girth and solidity of her blond sex-god's penis. Not wanting to appear timid, she reached for him, but when she circled her finger and thumb around his shaft, she could barely get them to meet.

Lukas gave her a smirking look.

Oh, you arrogant git! she thought. Fabulous as he was, he was just like any other man in this respect. Disgustingly proud of his dick and eager to shove it in the face of any eager woman. Ah well, in for a penny, in for a pound. Extending her tongue, she began to lick her way delicately around his shiny, circumcised glans.

A soft groan from Lukas told her that she was doing something right, so she worked her tongue harder, and in more energetic circular strokes, while caressing his shaft with both her hands at the same time. It was most unlikely that she could ever have given this man deep throat – even if she'd learned how to do it – but she was damn sure she was going to give him the best time she could. Furling her tongue to a point, she dove it mercilessly at his love-eye – and was rewarded by a sharp cry of pleasure and a lift of his hips.

Pre-ejaculate fluid began to flow into her mouth, and Clover lapped at it hungrily. Lukas really was the most delicious man she could possibly imagine – both figuratively and literally – and apart from the sheer pleasure of felating him, she experienced a heady rush of power. As much as was possible with her mouth full, she smiled in smug satisfaction and outright glee.

'Oh God, yes! Oh yes!' he chanted, his usually smooth American accent becoming more and more disjointed and ragged. How clichéd men were in expressing their pleasure, she thought. And even as she guessed more or less what she'd hear next, he gasped, 'Oh baby, baby, baby . . . Oh Jesus! Yes! I'm coming!'

The magnificent organ in her mouth leapt and jerked, and as he began to ejaculate, Lukas grabbed Clover's head between his two hands and forced her to take more of him. She gulped hard, but continued to suck gamely, swallowing the thick, creamy spurts of semen as it shot into her mouth. Through a haze of triumph, she felt his fingers gouge her scalp.

Lukas's paroxysms seemed to go on for an eternity, but in reality they couldn't have lasted for more than a few moments. Eventually he began to shrink and as daintily as she could, she allowed him to slip out from between her lips. In what she thought was a nice refinement, she licked the last vestiges of his come very gently off his fast declining flesh, then settled back on her heels to observe her fallen Adonis at bay.

Dirty boy, she thought with a grin, realising for the first time that there had been no sign of underpants or boxer shorts to impede her access to him. She wondered if Lukas always went commando, or whether he'd been so sure of himself today that he'd simply left his undies off for the occasion.

Clover frowned, watching Lukas stretch and grin like a satisfied cat. His eyes were closed as if he were still savouring the sensation. But he couldn't have known he'd meet me, surely? she thought. So why the state of readiness?

As Lukas's impossible lashes fluttered and he opened his eyes, Clover realised how silly she was being. Lukas must always be getting offers of sex – and she was just the lucky one who'd stumbled into his path today. And maybe he just didn't like wearing underwear? She could quite imagine that it was deliciously stimulating for a man to have his penis hanging free inside his jeans, being constantly caressed as he moved and walked around.

'What are you thinking about, Clover?'

Clover snapped out of it and became aware that she was still staring at the free-ranging dick in question. Flaccid now, it was still impressive, its width and sturdiness hinting at that eye-popping erection.

But even though she was thinking about his dick, Clover felt reluctant to say as much. Instead she got to her feet.

'Look, I don't know what the hell I'm doing here. I'm supposed to be delivering that portfolio to Olivia's button maker, and I told her I'd go straight there. Those sketches are precious and she doesn't have any copies.'

Lukas gave her a sardonic look, while neatly tucking his penis back into his jeans and zipping up. In spite of everything, Clover felt a pang of regret to see such a beautiful thing disappear.

'I thought we were having fun?' he said, buckling his belt. 'Don't you like the things I've taught you today? I thought you were a natural, Clover. A good sport. Game for anything.'

'I am! But I told Olivia I'd do something and I'd better do it. She's being very good to me. Letting me stay in her house rent free, meals and everything.'

Lukas looked at her more appraisingly this time, then smiled. 'You give great head, honey,' he said quite gently, 'but at heart you're a good girl, aren't you?'

'Not all that good!' retorted Clover indignantly. Oh yes, that was what her family and Roger had wanted her to be, but it wasn't what *she'd* wanted. And since she'd come to London, hadn't she been doing everything in her power, taking every weird opportunity presented to her, to ensure that she was as bad as she could possibly be?

'Don't worry,' said Lukas, rising smoothly to his feet with catwalk elegance. 'The good girls are always the best.'

'What do you mean?'

'They're much more fun to corrupt,' he gave her a broad, impish wink, 'and they always make the best bad girls in the end.'

Clover's heart quivered, and she experienced a hot feeling in her chest that sank almost immediately to her groin. She imagined some of the bad things she had yet to do, things she'd seen in Olivia's explicit books, and hoped beyond hope that Lukas might be the one to lead her through them. The most degrading act would be a blessing if he were the one to debauch her.

'Well, that's as may be, but Olivia will kill me if I don't get those drawings to the button maker. She's probably rung already to ask what he thinks.'

Glancing around, Clover wondered how much of an audience they'd had. At the time, she'd felt as if they were in a hermetic capsule, sealed away from the rest of the world, but now she realised that about a dozen people must have been enjoying quite a show.

Or maybe not?

In the far corner of the room, a young woman was bent over the back of one of the many leather Chesterfields while a rather elderly man – he must have been in his sixties, Clover thought – was thrusting into her slowly and regularly, with dogged determination. From the sheer effort that the aged roué was putting into the act, and the tortured grunts of his paramour, Clover got the distinct impression that he was buggering her rather than simply fucking her, and the idea of that made her pussy shudder empathically and her anus clench.

In another part of the room, an older woman of about forty-ish was standing on one of the coffee tables, her thighs parted in an ugly, splay-legged stance. All the clothing on the lower part of her body had been removed, apart from some rather dark and tarty-looking stockings, which had been rolled down to her knees, and she was masturbating vigorously, both hands between her legs. Whether this was her choice, or at the order of the three men who were sitting around the table drinking and casually chatting, Clover couldn't tell. But the woman's over-painted mouth was stopped with a large ball-gag jammed between her lips and held in place with a leather strap around the back of her head.

'Would you like to do that?' whispered Lukas from behind her. She felt him move close, pressing his long thigh against the back of her leg and her buttock, and, as he did so, he lifted her skirt from behind and pressed his finger against the lingering soreness from his spanks.

Clover hissed through her teeth. God, it still hurt so much, just from his hands. She began to wriggle though, when he slid the side of his hand between her bottom cheeks and began to rub it against her rosy vent.

'I want to do all sorts of things to you, Clover, you know that, don't you?' he murmured, fingering the tight little entrance again and again. 'I want to beat you and penetrate you in the nastiest ways. Exhibit you in front of a hundred lewd watchers with your holes stuffed and stretched wide open, everything wet and wanton and tormented.'

Clover nearly collapsed with longing. Her belly felt heavy again, her clit swollen just from hearing the outrageous words. She swayed on her feet and he slung an arm around her waist to hold her up, while with his other hand, he jammed two fingers into her vagina from behind.

'Do it . . . do it for me, baby,' he purred, almost lifting her off the ground, her weight on those two fingers, 'Do what she's doing. Bring yourself off. I know you want to come again.'

Speared by his fingers, and drugged by his husky transatlantic voice, Clover reached down, almost in a trance, and began to rub frantically at her clitoris. She was vaguely aware of people glancing idly in her direction, and even the eyes of the gagged woman upon her, but she cared nothing for any of them. She was completely in Lukas's thrall. Closing her eyes, she leaned back against him, frigged herself harder, and bore down on the digits lodged inside her.

'Good girl,' she heard him murmur. It was impossible not to move now, to jerk her hips and ride his hand to the rhythm of her own masturbation. She groaned as everything inside her seemed to freeze and tighten, then let out a high, sharp cry when it released again and she climaxed.

Enough already, she thought as she finally came to her senses again. She was standing in the middle of some perverted kind of gentlemen's club, her bare crotch dripping with her own juices and an American supermodel's fingers lodged in her vagina.

'Let me go, Lukas,' she said, trying to sound determined as she attempted to get up on her toes and wriggle free. 'I really do have to leave now.'

'You'll have to ask me nicer than that,' he said silkily, pushing his fingers deeper inside her. 'Getting snarky with me is no way to show your thanks.'

Clover felt a strange melting sensation which wasn't purely to do with physical responses. It was the game they were playing, a part of the great secret world, and it touched her psyche as much as it made her sex wet.

She was getting wetter again, which Lukas would readily be aware of. But she sensed he wanted resistance from her, so she pursed her lips and refused to answer him.

'Come on, honey, give me a pretty please,' he said softly, stirring his fingers inside her. There was something teasing in his voice now, conspiratorial, almost kindly. It might be a game and a power struggle, but he was a good man who respected all opponents.

Clover succumbed.

'Please, Lukas,' she said in a small but knowing voice, 'please will you take your fingers out of my pussy and let me leave now?'

'Pretty please?'

'Pretty please,' she gasped, feeling the heavy twitch of desire all over again.

In a smooth, deft movement he withdrew, then looked down at his hand contemplatively, slowly massaging her silkiness into his skin. When he seemed satisfied that all traces of her were absorbed, he looked up, gave her a mild, open, unchallenging smile, and said, 'Okay, sweetheart, shall we go?'

'At last!' God, for a man with whom she'd had the most exciting and kinky sex of her life he could be bloody exasperating! 'But I'll have my knickers back, if you please.' She stood in front of him, gazing boldly into his blue eyes, willing herself not to look away.

The smile became a seductive grin.

'Would you begrudge me a souvenir?' he said, reaching out to tuck away a wayward wisp of her hair. His gaze flicked up and down her body as if her crotch were still exposed and not safely hidden now that her skirt had dropped down into place. 'And besides, it's warm. Nobody needs underwear today.' He waggled his blond eyebrows, making her notice his one imperfection, which she'd only subliminally registered before. A scar marked his left brow and marred the symmetry of his face. It was slight, but she supposed that for photo shoots and the catwalk it was always masked by clever make-up.

'Lukas!' she cried when it became obvious that her panties weren't to be forthcoming.

'Pretty please?' he murmured, with a slow flick of his long lashes that bordered on blatantly camp.

'Oh, fuck you!' She turned and stomped away in the direction of the entrance hall, Isabel and the portfolio. It was alarming how draughty it felt without underwear, especially when her sex was still moist and sticky from her orgasms.

'I'd love you to.' With a couple of long strides, Lukas was at her side. 'But I thought you were in a hurry to deliver that portfolio?'

Clover said nothing, but she felt heat flare again in her face at a sudden image . . . Herself and Lukas in bed with her wrists handcuffed to the bed-head while he crouched between her thighs, licking her sex. Shaking inside she marched ahead, annoyed that Lukas could so effortlessly keep pace with her. People in the room were still watching them, seemingly as interested in their little tiff as they had been in the spanking and the blow-job and the masturbation . . .

Reaching the reception desk, Clover got a shock. It wasn't Isabel who emerged from the office door behind it, but a stunning young black man, exquisitely dressed in an immaculate morning suit.

'Hi, Jerome,' said Lukas amiably.

'Good afternoon, sir,' replied Jerome, before fixing Clover with a pleasant, attentive expression. 'How can I help you, madam?' he enquired.

Clover frowned, and felt the slow, almost nauseous stir of foreboding.

'Er . . . yes . . . I . . . When we came in, I left a large, black leather-covered portfolio at this desk. The woman on duty said she'd take care of it for me. Is she here? Could I have it, please?'

'Of course, madam, I'll look.'

Jerome graced her with another dazzling smile, then turned and disappeared into the office. Clover glanced across at Lukas and her stomach clenched in even deeper alarm. There was the oddest expression on his face, at once speculative, knowing and excited. He looked as if he were about to embark on some great adventure, something familiar, yet also thrilling to him. Without knowing why, Clover glanced down at his groin and suppressed a gasp when she saw that he had an erection again, swelling rapidly.

What the bloody hell was going on?

And the amount of time it was taking Jerome to find the portfolio only ramped up her anxiety. Surely it wasn't that hard to miss? It was big and the office was small, he should have been handing it to her by now.

But when the handsome young man returned, there was a regretful expression on his face.

'I'm sorry, Miss Weatherby, there's no portfolio here. Are you sure you left it?'

Without registering the fact that he seemed to have mysteriously learned her name, Clover darted forward and thrust her face towards Jerome's. 'But it *must* be there! It was only a short while ago! I gave it to the woman who was here before. To Isabel.' Her stomach was churning now. Olivia would be livid, and rightly so.

How could I let her down? thought Clover, darting around the desk and past the startled Jerome, to get into the small, neat office.

No portfolio. And nowhere for it to be hidden.

I should never have come here, she told herself, stomping out again, her thoughts whirling, wanting to blame Isabel, Jerome and mainly Lukas, but knowing it was her fault that her benefactress's precious designs had gone astray.

'Do you think Isabel might know where the portfolio is?' Lukas said, stepping forward and questioning Jerome. Clover looked at him, momentarily distracted.

What was it with him? He was asking politely, and with what sounded like genuine concern, but still there was that strange undercurrent. As if he were just going through the motions. And he still had that amazing hard-on in his jeans.

'I'm afraid Mrs Leeming has left for the day,' said Jerome, looking perplexed. 'And I know she's going away on holiday this afternoon, so we might not be able to reach her.'

Oh, how bloody convenient! Clover felt like shouting, but somehow, more and more, she knew that the portfolio just wasn't going to be found.

It had gone missing for a purpose, she realised in a sudden flash of illumination. It was all a subterfuge, part of a master-plan, a devious game.

And with a shudder in her heart and in her groin, she had a thrilling but terrible idea what that game might be.

And why it made Lukas's beautiful cock hard.

CHAPTER

10

C lover had expected fireworks when she told Olivia what had happened – and she got them.

'What the fucking hell did you think you were playing at? My designs are my livelihood! I entrusted them to you and what do you do? You bugger off somewhere with Lukas, without even telling me, and lose the bloody things!' Her eyes had flashed and her bosom had heaved spectacularly – and overly dramatically, Clover had suddenly thought. 'You do realise I'm going to lose an important contract now, don't you?'

Clover had nodded, a part of her quailing under the justified wrath of her benefactress, while another, strangely knowing part of her, applauded a bravura performance.

'What can I do to make it up to you?' she'd said.

Phone calls to Lukas and the club, so exclusive it didn't even have a name, were fruitless. Mrs Leeming, it seemed, had left for her holiday and couldn't be contacted, and no one else on the premises had even seen the portfolio.

After another tirade about ruined careers, and vicious rivals gloating over her demise, Olivia had pantomimed 'thinking about' Clover's offer so obviously that it'd taken a good deal of self-control not to laugh out loud.

She's playing me like a little fish on a hook, thought Clover, smiling inside, and she knows I know exactly what she's up to. Olivia was still doing her 'pondering' act, but any minute now, Clover knew the sting would come.

'There is something . . .' Olivia said hesitantly. 'But it's a bit . . . well . . . delicate.' She paused, then put on a stern face. 'But even so, you owe me big time, so I don't think you've any cause to make a fuss.'

'What is it? I'll do anything.' Clover was having a hard time playing along, but she managed it. Adhering to roles and putting on masks would soon be critically important, she sensed, and she might as well start now and learn the craft.

'Francis Black has taken a fancy to you,' Olivia said bluntly, smoothing her hair in a way that suggested, despite her tantrums, she might be nervous about this. 'He's having a house party over the Bank Holiday – a few like minded friends, to enjoy an "entertainment" – and I know he'd be extraordinarily grateful to me if I could persuade you to go along. It's his birthday, he'll be feeling generous and I might persuade him to offer me some backing.' She gave Clover a fierce look. 'Which might go some way to compensating me for the contract I've no doubt lost because of you!'

'But I'll go anyway, Olivia. If I'm asked. I don't need

coercing.' Clover continued to feign insouciance, even though her heart was pounding and she suddenly felt acutely sexually excited.

Olivia hesitated. 'But you wouldn't just be an ordinary guest. Francis would want you to play a special role.' Clover watched her swallow, and observed a strange expression cross the older woman's face. A sort of envy, and a reflection of the gathering lust she herself was feeling.

'What kind of role?' Clover asked, although she already knew. She watched the continued play of emotions in Olivia's beautiful features.

'I can't really tell you. Francis wouldn't like it. It spoils the effect.'

'Then why should I go to this party knowing nothing? It all sounds very fishy to me.'

Olivia rounded on her in fury. Or mock fury . . . 'Think of what you owe me, young lady! What you've jeopardised . . . I think a few days out of your life is the least you can offer to compensate me, don't you? You could have screwed up my business reputation for years to come!'

'Well, when you put it like that . . .' Clover pinned a penitent expression on her face, containing her laughter with some difficulty, 'of course I'll do it. You're right, what's a few days? I'll probably enjoy it.'

I *know* I'll enjoy it, she thought later, lying in bed, wondering what she'd let herself in for. She was aware in broad terms that the house party would be like some kind of extension of the evening gathering Olivia had taken her to. People would be punished, exposed, humiliated; there would be a lot of sex, most of it kinky and probably with a variety of partners.

But what exactly would her 'special role' entail?

Closing her eyes and throwing off the bedclothes, Clover stirred restlessly. It was a hot night, and the thoughts that began to drift through her mind were even hotter.

Would *she* be punished? Hell, yes, probably! It was more a question of how much she'd be punished, by whom, and could she take it?

Wriggling against the sheets and feeling sweat trickle in her armpits and her groin, she reached around and touched her bottom, stirring the faint, fading soreness from the spanking Lukas had given her.

God, it had hurt! It had hurt so much more than she'd ever expected. And yet, lying there, she found herself craving it again. Wishing she was back there across his lap with her buttocks on fire and her sex engorged and dripping, just ready for his touch.

Sliding her fingers between her legs, she found she was wet and swollen in reality.

Oh, Lukas, she thought dreamily, sliding two fingers inside herself and wishing they were his. It'd been so shaming the way he'd penetrated her like that, and yet it had excited her almost to madness. And the fact that there had been watchers, too, had roused her blood and made her want to do more, endure more, show more. She almost wished he'd made her lift her leg and exhibit her sex to all the occupants of that dark, discreet room. She imagined putting on a performance, writhing and moaning, jerking her hips, drawing attention to her pussy, speared as it was by Lukas's long, tapered fingers.

'Oh God,' gasped Clover, feeling her own fingertips slip and slide across her sex. She wanted to do more now, to be ruder, as if she were practising for the plea-sures and ordeals ahead. Pulling at her pyjama bottoms, she stripped them off, then wrenched open her top, popping off a button. Scrambling to a sitting position, she reached into the drawer, then peered in, studying the selection of sex toys Olivia had so thoughtfully provided for her.

Ticklers, love-eggs, nipple clamps and strange vibra-tors with attachments that looked like little birds and animals; it was quite a treasure-trove. But she was not in the mood for decisions. Clover pulled out a modestly sized and rather plain vibrator made of red plastic. Without pausing to hesitate she pushed it inside herself, and tried to imagine that it was Lukas.

Of course, he was bigger than the humble sex toy, but closing her eyes again, Clover let her imagination embellish the sensations.

He was thrusting, going at her like a train, shagging her senseless. She could almost see his beautiful face, feel his long-fingered hands grasping her freshly spanked buttocks, igniting the flames of pain, hear him gasping obscenities and promises of new depravities.

The scene changed to her hanging in chains while Lukas whipped her. He was using that heavy, silver-buckled leather belt of his, swinging it with all his considerable strength; beating her while she whined and begged for mercy.

She had no idea what the belt would feel like against her flesh, but she knew it would be awesome. And her body already intuited the effect it would have upon her. Deep in the quick of her, her womb pulsed hungrily, and, finding her clitoris with frantic fingers, she began to rub. And rub and rub . . .

Imagining the kiss of Lukas's belt, she climaxed heavily.

'So, has our little friend taken the bait? Has she agreed to be our plaything at Francis's birthday orgy?'

Olivia nodded. She couldn't see Circe's face, but she could imagine her smug, gleeful expression. And she hoped passionately that Francis would not put Clover into Circe's less than tender hands. The dark-haired beauty could be crueller than any man when she had the devil in her, as Olivia's abused back and bottom could silently attest.

She was standing in the corner of Circe's sybaritic crimson bedroom, with her hands on her head, and her body striped with weals just as rosy as the painted silk wall-coverings. She was in thrall to Circe for the moment, and when the Hispanic woman had phoned her in the middle of the night and summoned her, Olivia had had no choice but to obey and rush to Circe's apartment – to be dealt with.

First, Circe had ordered her to strip naked, drop to her knees and lick her black patent stiletto heels until they were spotless. Then, Olivia had had to walk out on to Circe's balcony, stand with her thighs apart, and play with herself for the delectation of anyone who might be observing her across the nearby rooftops. At first Olivia had been shaking, and deeply embarrassed. It was one thing to bring herself off among friends, but for total strangers, in the outdoors? However, very quickly, she'd begun to get excited and very wet between her legs.

But just as she'd started the delicious rise to orgasm, Circe had joined her on the balcony and fetched her a vicious slap across the face, calling her a slut.

After that, Olivia had been hauled across the back of a chaise longue in Circe's bedroom, and whipped with a switch until she shouted and howled. Now she was confined to the corner, unable to see anything, but fully able to hear groans and purrs and rustlings, as Circe lay on her wide, silk-sheeted bed and masturbated.

'So? Has she?' Circe reiterated, her voice rasping with lust. 'You may speak now.'

Big of you, thought Olivia, suppressing a twinge of resentment. Even though she found Circe utterly desirable, and adored the erotic games they played together, there were times when the real world, and their natural business rivalry reared its head. And sometimes, too, she thought that Circe went just a bit over the top with the dominant mistress act. The woman didn't know the meaning of subtlety.

'Yes. Yes, she has,' Olivia said in a low, respectful voice. She might as well play along. After all, she had agreed to be Circe's 'slave'. 'But I suspect she's fully aware of the implications. She seems knowing beyond her limited experience, somehow. As if she might be a natural for the scene.'

'Excellent!' cried Circe huskily. 'I look forward to testing her. She has a very beautiful body. I'd like to get my hands on it.'

Olivia felt a pang of alarm, and felt strongly tempted to turn around. 'But isn't Lukas going to initiate her? She seems to have formed a bond with him. It might be . . . um . . . kinder to let him ease her into things if she likes him.'

'You're too soft!' Circe's voice was stern, even though Olivia could tell the other woman was getting close to orgasm. The sound of writhing movement on the bed

145

was more pronounced now, and she could imagine Circe's slender legs akimbo as she rubbed frantically at her freshly shaven pussy.

'Francis will let me have a turn with her,' the dark woman went on. 'I'm sure of it. I only have to talk nicely to him and promise a special show.'

I'll have to be there too, thought Olivia, trying to concentrate on a strategy, but finding the show being put on here was becoming too distracting. She couldn't see what Circe was doing, but her mind presented her with the perfect picture.

Circe's thighs wide open, her fingers, tipped with crimson nail polish, at work between her sex lips, toying with the tiny rosy button of her clitoris. Slick juices would be shining on her swollen labia, dripping from the entrance to her vagina. Olivia's mouth watered as she imagined herself there, supping the musky fluids and caressing the puffy membranes with her tongue.

The chime of the doorbell fractured her fantasy and obviously Circe's concentration too. The other woman roared with annoyance and cursed volubly in Spanish.

'Who the fuck can that be at this time of night?' she cried, clearly frustrated at having her orgasm snatched from her.

Olivia had no idea, but she suspected that it might be one of their 'circle'. After all, who else would come visiting during the hours when most people were sleeping?

'Answer the door, slave!' commanded Circe, after a moment, her tone no longer angry but full of mischievous imperiousness.

Olivia let her hands drop from her head and turned round. She reached for her clothes, which were thrown haphazardly across a chair, but Circe stopped her with another arrogant order.

'No! As you are!'

Olivia swallowed, part of her wanting to protest, but most of her feeling a rush of anticipation at the prospect of exhibiting her naked body again to a total stranger, or to some like-minded friend. She imagined opening the door, and seeing the newcomer's eyes widen and darken with lust at the sight of her large breasts, their nipples currently rouged to Circe's order, and her carefully shaven bush. And the *coup de grâce* would be if she turned around, bent over, and displayed her voluptuous bottom, complete with its adornment of reddened stripes.

What would a stranger think of the marks of her punishment?

'Of course,' she murmured, crossing the room, aware of the way her high heels made her hips sway and her large breasts bounce lightly with each step. Her current slave status meant that she shouldn't really look at Circe, her mistress, but she caught a quick glance of the other woman nevertheless.

Circe was playing with herself again, her momentary distraction obviously forgotten. She had one leg elegantly raised, folded at the knee, and her hips tilted a little. With one hand she was caressing her clit, circling it in a slow, lazy, but purposeful action with one finger; the other hand was beneath her, delicately fondling her anus. She was the very image of total debauchery, and Olivia wanted her.

She made her way through the flat to the door. Her nipples tightened as she walked. It had to be somebody Circe knew and trusted because there was a security code in the lobby. She unlatched and unbolted the door and let it swing open.

'Hello, Ollie, this is a pleasure. Is Circe in?' said Nathan Ribiero, his dark, widened eyes skittering from her breasts to her belly and to her groin. He was clad in a weather-beaten denim shirt and equally aged jeans, and looked decidedly edible, his swarthy young face flushed with lust.

It was only when Nathan had feasted his eyes on all her attractions that he glanced pointedly at the slim, black leather collar Olivia wore around her throat.

'Oh, it's like that, is it?' he said, grinning widely, obviously pleased by her status. Reaching out, he grabbed a breast and kneaded it, as he was entitled to when she wore the badge of subservience, his other hand going straight to her crotch and groping it roughly.

Denied an orgasm by Circe, Olivia couldn't help but moan and lean hard on Nathan's fingers. He gripped her cruelly, both above and below, and she felt her innards gather themselves, shuddering and rising rapidly to pleasure. When he manoeuvred her and pushed her against the wall, and began kissing her savagely, tongue halfway down her throat, she couldn't help herself and climaxed almost immediately, the pleasure winding itself around the pain from her injured bottom banging against the plasterwork.

'You're a dirty, wicked woman, Ollie,' Nathan growled amiably as he pulled away. 'I bet Circe won't be too pleased that you've thrown yourself at me to grab a quick orgasm, will she?'

Olivia hung her head. She'd come once, but her sex was hungry and it clamoured for more and more.

'Will she?' demanded Nathan, swinging her around and looking at her reddened buttocks. 'Ah, I see she's done a number on you already.' He pinched the wounded flesh and Olivia whimpered, feeling her pussy gush with juice.

'N-no, she's ... she's been keeping me on the edge ... I wasn't allowed to come,' she gasped, wanting to thrust herself against Nathan and come again, rubbing herself against his sturdy, denim-clad thigh.

'Well, let's go and see what she thinks about it, shall we?' With a soft, gleeful laugh, Nathan closed his fingers tightly around Olivia's left bottom cheek, and used his grip on it to manhandle her forward towards Circe's bedroom.

When they reached their destination, they found Circe jerking and grunting in the throes of her own orgasm. Her eyes were closed and both hands were hard at work, fore and aft. They stood together for a few moments watching her, Nathan's hand roving rudely over Olivia's body, eagerly revisiting her breasts, her bottom and the slippery wet channel between her legs.

Eventually, the dark beauty slumped back amongst her pillows, her chest heaving and a cat-like smile on her exotic, olive-skinned face. Her eyes flicked open.

'Good evening, Nathan, what brings you here?' she said pleasantly, sitting up and taking a healthy swig from the glass of wine on her bedside table. As she swallowed, her eyes followed the movements of Nathan's hands as he continued to grope Olivia.

For her part, Olivia found herself rising above the insistent pleasure and looking closely at her dramatic friend's dark, slanted eyes. Circe had a new agenda, she was sure of it. The expression on the other woman's face was subtle, but it was there. Olivia doubted that the impetuous, greedy Nathan would be aware of it – he always grabbed what he wanted and thought of nothing but a single goal – but she could see it and it excited her as much as the moving fingers at her crotch.

'What's this house party that Francis is giving? When is it? Am I invited?' He pinched Olivia's nipple and twisted it, as if blaming her for his lack of an invitation.

'It's his birthday bash,' said Circe coolly, rising from her bed, her filmy wrap floating around her. It hid nothing, but then it wasn't intended to. 'Just select friends abd a few days of sensual entertainment – the usual thing. I'm surprised he hasn't contacted you.'

'No, he hasn't!' Nathan said peevishly, jamming several fingers into Olivia's vagina, making her rise on her toes. She gasped, feeling her body responding to the rough treatment, but almost laughing too.

Circe's dark eyes drifted over Olivia, then returned to Nathan. 'Why not fuck her?' she suggested casually, then nodded towards the chair over which, earlier, Olivia had taken her thrashing. 'Take her from behind. I'd like to watch that.'

'Right on!' said Nathan softly, pushing Olivia across the room, his fingers still inside her. He dragged them out peremptorily and tossed her across the chair's upholstered back.

A moment later, Olivia heard the sound of a zip, Nathan shedding his clothing, then felt the head of his impressive dick start pushing into her sex. She was so wet and so ready that he slid in easily, and a second later she was climaxing.

'Dirty slut,' he growled, slapping her hard across her

punished buttocks and making her come even more fiercely.

'About this house party,' he went on, almost immediately beginning to thrust into her in a fast greedy rhythm. His voice shook every time he shoved. 'Can you get me an invitation? I really want to be there. I hear he's having a new slave broken in and he's going to exhibit her.'

Olivia looked up, and caught Circe's eye. The other woman was reaching into a drawer in her dressing table, and after a second or two, she brought out a familiar object.

'Perhaps *we* could take you, Nathan,' Circe murmured archly, 'as a guest . . . or maybe . . .'

When Olivia glanced into the dressing-table mirror, she saw that Nathan had his eyes closed and a hungry, intent expression on his face as he fucked her. He hadn't seen what Circe now had in her hand.

Olivia grinned, as Circe sidled around behind them and laid a hand encouragingly on his backside. Nathan didn't open his eyes.

'Oh yeah,' he panted, throwing his all into her. Olivia winced with the impact against her stripes of pain, and tried not to laugh as she watched Circe in the mirror. The other woman winked at her, then made a swift, deft movement.

'What?' Nathan choked, as the thin band of leather – the slave collar – went around his neck, and Circe quickly buckled it into place.

'You could go as our guest,' she said, sounding utterly pleased with herself, 'but I'd much prefer it, and Olivia would too, if you went as our slave. It's a grand debauch, my sweet. Only *one* slave as entertainment just

151

isn't going to be enough.' With that, she hooked a finger through the collar at the back and ungently hauled the gasping, protesting Nathan away from Olivia.

'You ... you can't do this!' he cried. But Circe was stronger than she looked, and to Olivia's knowledge, was proficient in several forms of martial arts.

'Oh yes, I can, my boy! I've had my instructions. You either comply with this, or you leave the circle and never return to it. That's your choice. You have to learn some humility before you progress further.'

Olivia straightened up. She was disappointed that such a vigorous, if demeaning, fuck was over, but it didn't really matter. Circe was magnificent when she was in high dominatrix mode, and even better when you weren't the one she was dominating. Olivia glanced at her friend, and was unsurprised when Circe nodded slightly, indicating that she remove her own collar. Slipping it off, she crossed the room, sidled up to Circe and kissed her, relishing the look of shock and alarm that had transformed Nathan's handsome young face. His prick had subsided too, but that could soon be remedied she thought with a smile as she began to caress Circe's breast.

Once they started punishing him, he'd soon get a hard-on again ... and with careful handling they could both use his fine young body for their pleasure.

'What will it be, Milady Circe?' she murmured archly, giving her friend's lush breast a last squeeze before she crossed to the carved Spanish chest where Circe stored her choice collection of corporal punishment paraphernalia. 'Shall we try the crop today? Or will it be the cane?'

As Nathan moaned, she saw his cock was rising

again. His face was a picture of woe and confusion now, and to her surprise, she could swear she saw the glitter of tears in his eyes. Did he have it in him to endure? she wondered. To go through the barrier of suffering and reach the strange, sublime state where pain became pleasure, and each stroke of the crop, the lash or the cane was a prize to be sought instead of a punishment to fear?

He's very headstrong, she thought, very wilful. Even though he looked scared, she could also see that he was already getting impatient. Circe was obviously aware of this, which was why she seemed to be taking her time.

'I'll take a paddle,' she said at length, 'but first, I think, a little play, then perhaps a little hand spanking.' She spun towards Nathan, fixing him with a beady glare. 'What a pathetic example of manhood you are, young Nathan. One little scare and you've got a dick like an earthworm.' She strode over to him, her flimsy robe floating around her, her lithe limbs flashing and inspiring a new jolt of lust in Olivia's loins.

'It's just not good enough!' the Hispanic woman went on, frowning at Nathan's penis, even though it was beginning to rise. 'I want that at a full stand! Come on, you little creep, do something about it!' In a lightning movement she slapped him full across the face.

'But—' he protested.

Circe slapped him again, and this time, he began to cry. Olivia found herself feeling sorry for him. But that didn't stop her rush of glee when she drew out the paddle and his wet eyes widened.

'This! Erect! Now!' commanded Circe, flipping his half-hard manhood unmercifully with the back of her hand.

Obediently, Nathan began to pull at himself, masturbating clumsily while his eyes flicked from the baleful Circe, to Olivia and the paddle, and back again. Within seconds he was fiercely erect, his hard dick red and glistening with pre-come and the residue from being recently inside Olivia.

'Enough!' cried Circe. 'Now make it dance!'

Nathan looked confused for a moment, and yelped when Circe struck him across the face again.

'Make it dance,' she ordered, her voice soft this time, but somehow far more menacing.

Revelation dawned on his face and he whimpered in horror and shame. Circe gave him a fierce look and his bottom lip wavering, he began to move his hips.

Olivia bit her lip and hid a huge grin, as her lover's cock began to sway and wave about in time to his gyrations. He looked ludicrous, like an inept male belly dancer, his swollen organ bobbing up and down, its reddened tip dancing in circles. She wondered what the drag and lurch of that huge bar of flesh felt like to him, and imagined it was somehow more agonising even than the bite of the lash against his bottom. And she could certainly believe that the shame was greater than the ache.

'Faster!' instructed Circe, but unlike Olivia she made no effort to hide her amusement. She laughed, as Nathan's penis bounced and swung through the air.

Tears were streaming down the young man's face now, and he was clenching his fists at his side as he moved. Olivia had no way of knowing whether this was in anger or in mortification, but his face was now uniformly red, not just where Circe had slapped him.

'Do you think you can you hit a moving target,

Ollie?' said Circe suddenly, flashing a teasing glance towards Olivia.

Olivia couldn't contain her own mirth now. 'I can certainly try, Milady Circe,' she said, swishing the paddle experimentally through the air once or twice.

Focus! she thought, watching the movements of Nathan's bare bottom. A second later, she caught his rhythm and spanked him hard across the crown of one cheek, making him shout out piteously and incoherently, and jerk his hips even more.

'Oh nooo!' he keened, as she got into the swing of things, fetching him a series of square-on, satisfying blows that rapidly reddened both lobes of his bottom. Pretty soon, he abandoned his demeaning dance, his hands flew to his prick and he began masturbating.

'If you continue with that,' Circe purred warningly, 'it'll be all the worse for you. Have a care, young Nathan, have a care.'

But Nathan continued pumping himself and almost immediately, with a gurgling cry and a paroxysm of juddering hips, he ejaculated copiously, long strings of pale semen shooting out of him.

There was a long silence, punctuated only by Nathan's gasps and sobs. He was crying freely now, his face a poignant picture of pain, shame, pleasure and a shining enlightenment.

'Too bad, little man, you've let us down,' said Circe softly, crossing behind him to the box of implements. 'I'm afraid we're going to have to take things a little more seriously from now on.' From the box, she drew out a leather strap, thick, black and heavy. She nodded to Olivia, 'Why don't you have a rest, Ollie dear? I'll take over from here.'

As Circe advanced on Nathan, and led him, snivelling, to the back of the chair, where she pushed him face down across it, Olivia lay down on the bed and pressed her own wounds of pleasure against the coverlet. Hissing through her teeth, she turned on to her side, for a better view.

As the first blow fell and Nathan screamed, she slid her fingers between her legs and began to rub.

CHAPTER

11

C lover smoothed down the flimsy skirt of her aubergine suit, and scanned the street again, hoping and praying the car would come for her soon. Her heart was leaping and she felt vulnerable and exposed.

'I can't tell you. I can't tell you,' Olivia had said again and again in answer to her questions about the days that lay ahead, and after a while Clover had simply stopped asking. But that hadn't quelled the anticipation – or the fear.

This is preposterous, she thought, feeling draughts whistle up her thighs and make her grateful that she was at least allowed knickers. I shouldn't let myself be manoeuvred like this. It's blatant sexual exploitation. I must be insane. I should either pack my bags and head home, or I should confront Olivia and tell her I bloody well know that her stupid portfolio isn't lost, and that all this is just a ruse to procure her friends a willing plaything. God knows, that was probably the only reason she invited me to stay with her in the first place.

But Clover knew she wouldn't do either of those things. It was an unreal situation, but in her heart and her gut and her crotch, she wanted it. When that car came for her, she wouldn't just be stepping into its luxurious back seat, she'd be stepping through the mirror into the secret world again.

But will Lukas be there to meet me? she wondered.

That was her only qualm. Her beautiful blond god was inextricably entangled with the new world. He was the very symbol of its mystery and power. Oh, she knew there would be many others within its boundaries who would pleasure her as well as use and abuse her, but no one else was on quite the same level.

And this uncertainty was the only real reason that she was considering cutting and running, and dashing back upstairs to the safety of Olivia's flat.

Too late!

Threading efficiently through the traffic came the same car that she and Olivia had ridden in on the night of that first party. And when it drew up to the curb, it was Damian the chauffeur who again leaped out to assist her into the discreet, leather-scented seclusion of its palatial back seat. He made no comment on her lack of luggage – Olivia had told her that she'd be given everything she needed when she got there – but simply said, 'Good afternoon, Miss Weatherby, just make yourself comfortable.'

Clover remembered the last time she'd ridden in this car: her nervousness, Olivia touching herself, Damian watching them. This time though, the chauffeur seemed to be applying his entire attention to the road and the London traffic. He didn't speak to her once they were under way.

I don't even know where this place is, thought Clover, her heart still pounding. In fact it was beating even more furiously now the journey had actually begun. How long was she going to sit alone in this car, her anticipation and anxiety ratcheting ever upwards?

Not long, it seemed, because the limousine suddenly began to slow, then pulled up to wait in front of an upmarket apartment building with a quietly elegant façade and a livery clad doorman.

Who were they waiting for? Some other attendee at the revel? Maybe even Francis Xavier Black himself? How would she maintain a conversation with whoever it was, she wondered, given her status? Maybe she wouldn't have to. Perhaps the 'entertainment' was about to begin already.

But Clover's spirits soared when a tall, familiar figure emerged from the foyer and paused to exchange a few words and a smile with the doorman. As he left the shade of the building's canopy, the bright afternoon sun struck Lukas's dazzling white-gold hair and made it glitter like the halo of an angel, and his fluid, rangy stride set his long black coat billowing around him like Dracula's cloak. His face was impassive, but his eyes were unnaturally brilliant.

The impression of a dark prince was further reinforced by the way Damian rushed from the car and darted around to open the rear passenger door for Lukas. He all but doffed his cap, and Clover was convinced she saw genuine awe in his face.

'Hello—' Clover began, only to have the words stopped by Lukas's long, elegant forefinger against her lips.

'Don't speak,' he said in a soft but determined tone. 'From now on, you don't utter a word unless you're invited. From now on, Clover, you have no will and no rights. You are simply a body for the use of others, those who have already earned their place in the circle.' He gave her a steady, unblinking look, his astonishing eyes like blue fire in the shaded interior of the car. 'Do you understand me?'

Shaking, Clover nodded. The situation was nothing more than she'd expected, really, but to hear it spelled out made her feel so excited she was almost light-headed.

No will. No rights.

Oh God, what were they going to do to her? She wasn't really afraid in the deepest pathological sense, more scared she wouldn't acquit herself well, that she'd disappoint these people who'd gone before her into this world she so longed to enter. She felt a deep anxiety – most of all – that she would let down this beautiful man who sat beside her, who'd come to mean so much to her.

'Good girl. That's a start,' he said quietly, evenly. There was still no discernible expression on his face; he looked just as he did on the catwalk, exquisite, but emotionless. Deep in his eyes, however, Clover saw something that made her heart sing. There was a smile, together with warmth and encouragement. She sensed that even though the protocols of this strange situation didn't allow him to show it, he was on her side, he wanted her to succeed, and he would help her. Even if he had to appear pitiless and cruel to do it.

Bring it on! she thought wildly. Bring on everything. Do your worst. I can take it!

For a few seconds more, Lukas regarded her from behind his mask of perfection, then with just one blink of his long eyelashes he turned away and looked out of the window.

Clover did not feel downcast by his silence. In fact, his strong stillness beside her set every nerve tingling. Lukas was here, and she had an excited premonition that he was going to continue to be with her . . .

What if he's my tutor, or my guard? My keeper? My mentor?

Drawing in a delicious lungful of his exotic, spicy cologne, she found her body rousing almost painfully at the thought of what lay ahead, and what Lukas might be called on to do to her. The spanking he'd given her at the mysterious gentlemen's club was probably nothing, a mere pinprick. She thought of what he'd said to her, what he'd threatened her with and her mind and her body went into overdrive.

She wanted to be naked, now, and to abase herself to him. She wanted to open herself, play with herself for him. To push things inside her body, to be filled with shame, to crawl on the floor of this deluxe car, shuffle between Lukas's legs and suck his dick again.

What would happen if she just did it? Would he punish her for her impetuosity? Or would he allow her access to his marvellous body? Maybe it would be both?

Her heart bouncing like a steam-hammer against her ribcage, she reached out and laid her hand upon his thigh.

Retribution was instant. Lukas's hand shot out to

knock hers away, then before she could even gasp, he whipped up her skirt and slapped her hard and painfully across her inner thigh.

Clover whimpered at the pain of it, but felt a gush of juice drench the gusset of her panties.

'You're wilful, Clover,' he said almost conversationally, glancing at her as if she were a child who'd just attempted to steal a lollipop, 'and that little performance is going to cost you dearly ... eventually.' He continued to stare at her coolly, his blue eyes level and bright as stars.

Clover felt as if her heart were going to burst. Her nipples were pushing hard against the inside of her lace bra, and her clitoris and labia were swollen and engorged. She wanted to touch herself now, and wondered if she dare do it.

For a few moments, all she heard was the sound of their breathing: hers heavy and gasping; Lukas's perfectly even. Then he said, 'Take off your panties.'

Clover obeyed, and immediately Lukas took them from her.

'Lift your skirt, then press yourself down against the seat. I want you to feel the leather against your sex and your anus. Use your fingers to spread yourself, so everything's in contact.'

Clover stifled a moan, but followed his instructions. The delicate membranes of her pussy fluttered as she bore down, and the contact between the naked rosebud of her nether opening and the cool hide made her feel rude and wanton and fidgety. She wanted to wriggle about, rock against the pressure, but she knew that, until given permission, such an action was taboo.

'Now, place your hands on the seat beside you,

162

palms upwards, and keep them there. No moving.'

Again, Clover silently complied. Then she felt her eyes bug and her belly clench in protest when Lukas reached out, prised open her lips and carefully inserted the wadded up lace bundle of her panties into her mouth.

Clover groaned behind her makeshift gag, the taste of her own essence pungent on her tongue and in her throat. She felt her face turning crimson with mortification, and yet still her sex pulsed hungrily and wept more fluid on to the leather of the seat.

Oh, please touch me, she pleaded silently, not daring to look at Lukas. He was unattainable again, and she was just the lowest of the low; a slave, a plaything.

Desire ripped her to shreds, whirling round her body in violent motion, even though she was sitting as still as still could be. She'd never felt more turned on, or hungrier for even the tiniest crumb of stimulation. But there was nothing but the cool touch of the leather against her burning hot furrow. As discreetly as she could, she pressed down harder, trying to rock herself against the seat without it being apparent to Lukas.

'Have a care, little one,' he said softly, and when Clover risked a swift glance at him, she realised that he was watching her closely. Lounging against deep upholstery, he was as relaxed and elegant as a cat, yet he was nevertheless as completely aware of her as she was of him. And his face might still bear all the impassivity of classical Grecian statuary, but even he couldn't hide the dilation of his pupils and fervid glitter in his eyes.

You want me, don't you, Goldilocks? she taunted him in her head, drawing strength from his arousal.

For a while, they journeyed in silence, cocooned in

the dark, luxurious capsule of the car. Even Damian was excluded from their intense world, as Lukas had wound up the privacy barrier between themselves and the chauffeur.

Clover looked out of the window, but saw nothing. She could see only pictures in her mind of the possible scenarios that lay ahead, each one more and more lurid and perverted. She wished she could stop because with each new scene her body became more uncomfortable, her clitoris more engorged, her sex heavier and more aching with need.

Eventually, Lukas spoke, making her jump in her seat.

'We're nearly there,' he said calmly. 'Time to get ready. You'd better remove your skirt, slave.'

Without thinking, Clover tried to protest, but the panties in her mouth muffled the sound, and all she uttered was an uncouth gurgle.

'Please do as I say,' Lukas persisted in a quiet, unconcerned voice, 'or I'll be forced to do it for you and punish you for your lack of co-operation.'

Fumbling with the zip and the placket, Clover managed to unfasten her skirt and then slide it off. Lukas took it from her and tossed it casually on the seat beside him, not even bothering to look at what she'd exposed by its removal.

Without the benefit of a slip, Clover was naked from the waist down, apart from her sheer hold-up stockings. Belly, crotch, and when she stood up, buttocks; all were completely on show. She felt almost sick with anxiety and anticipation.

He was going to parade her like this ... but in front of whom? Her vagina clenching, Clover imagined a crowd. A mass of lewdly observing revellers, just as there'd been at Francis's party, all ogling her groin and her bottom . . . perhaps even reaching out to touch and sample the goods.

Clover's heart rose into her throat, as the car slowed before a pair of high, wrought-iron gates. Although Damian did nothing to announce their arrival, a second or two later, the gates swung slowly open, allowing them to pass through into large, park-like gardens and proceed along a neatly groomed gravel drive, at the far end of which, Clover could see an imposing classical house. There was a broad terrace in front of the house's porticoed doors, and even from a distance she could see a party. People were gathered, drinking and enjoying the afternoon sunshine . . . and soon they'd be enjoying the floorshow too.

This was the audience for her semi-naked display.

'Don't worry. This will make it better.'

She whirled towards Lukas just in time to see him drawing a black silk scarf from the pocket of his coat, then almost instantaneously, the world went dark as he tied it over her eyes.

'But I'll fall,' she tried to protest through the obstructing cloth in her mouth, the sound ugly and pathetic. Thinking of her high heels, her fear doubled when she felt him reach behind her, take one of her hands, then cuff it firmly to the other.

'You've nothing to fear,' Lukas murmured in her ear. 'I'll be with you, I'll guide you.'

Her heart bashed against her chest, but, strangely, his words calmed her. He was strong; he would catch her if she fell.

Once out on the gravel, she nearly stumbled, but

Lukas supported her effortlessly and she was able to walk. The warm sun caressed her naked belly and buttocks, making her doubly aware of her nudity. She felt a thin trickle of juice slide down the inside of her thigh and dampen the top of her stocking.

Murmurs of appreciation rippled across the terrace.

'Oh, very nice,' said one voice, a man, sounding happy and frankly lustful.

'What a beautiful bottom,' remarked a woman, almost lazily. 'But it'll look better when it's red and sore, perhaps a little swollen.'

'Didn't I promise you a treat?' Clover recognised Francis Black's voice, 'It's my birthday,' he continued indulgently, 'and yet it's my guests who are getting the gifts.'

'Gifts?' queried someone, sounding excited.

'A male slave should be arriving shortly,' Francis went on. 'That is, if a certain two dear friends haven't decided to keep him for themselves.'

A male slave? Who? thought Clover, sharing the surge of interest.

But her speculations were interrupted when Lukas whispered in her ear, 'There are two steps now. Lean on me; I'll get you up them.'

And with no effort, or trips on her part, he did. 'All flat going from here on in,' he murmured, taking her more firmly by the arm and propelling her forward into the throng of the gathered party guests.

As she stood in their midst, her worst fears and deepest, strangest hopes were realised. A man's hand, with thick, callused fingers, grabbed her between the legs and began to knead and explore.

'My God, Lukas, she's a dirty little bitch, isn't she?'

the unknown groper said with a low laugh. 'She's sopping wet. What have you been doing to her?' The fingers moved more insultingly, poking at her labia and flicking at her clit. She moaned into her wadded panties when her vagina pulsed lightly in response.

Lukas said nothing, but she felt him shrug against her, and sensed his smile, knowing and non-committal. Maybe he wouldn't have admitted to touching her even if he had? It was possible that he too was operating under some kind of dictate from Francis Black. Possible, even, that if he mishandled the slave in his custody, he too could end up being punished.

'Now, now, Harry, share and share alike,' another male voice said, and the first hand was reluctantly withdrawn. 'Let's get her up on the table here. I'd like to get a better look at this delicious little quim of hers.'

Before she could even draw breath, Clover found herself being lifted into the air in Lukas's strong arms. She felt an unbearable desire to throw her arms around him and nestle into the safety and security of his chest, but there was no chance. She was placed on her back on what felt like a wrought-iron garden table, her thighs roughly drawn wide apart and her cuffed hands wedged uncomfortably beneath her.

For a few seconds, she felt the sun beating down on her naked sex, then hands and fingers were upon her again. This time the examination was insulting. Her labia were pulled and stretched as if her privates were a horse's mouth being inspected for age and condition. Her legs were pushed even further open and the cushions from a couple of garden chairs placed under her bottom, then the inspection went on.

Ungentle fingers pushed at her orifices, making her

groan in shamed response. She got the impression that there was more than one person probing her now. She was roughly penetrated in both vagina and anus, and held in a pincer-like grip, while another finger and thumb grasped her clitoris tightly and began to tug at it in a jerky rhythm.

Oh no! she thought, gobbling and drooling around the obstruction in her mouth, as her sex began to react of its own accord, the response divorced from her appalled mind. She jerked and flailed beneath the ministrations of the intruding hands, her loins imploding into pleasure even as tears of shame trickled from beneath her black silk blindfold. Her body gripped and embraced the fingers lodged in her vagina and her bottom, just as if they were penises and they belonged to an adored lover. She imagined Lukas watching her immolation and her body clenched in another huge, wrenching orgasm.

Then, as suddenly as they'd violated her, the fingers were gone, and she heard an excited, lust-roughened voice cry, 'She's a wilful little whore. She should be punished for that. Right now!'

But the cool tones of Francis Black cut through the sudden mêlée of voices demanding her punishment.

'All in good time, friends,' he said expansively. 'There will be plenty of opportunities to observe her under the lash. But for now, I think, a shower is in order. She smells of sweat and sex and she needs cleaning up.' He paused, as if listening to the sudden sounds of assent. 'Could you see to that, Lukas? I know she's in the best of hands with you.'

Again, Lukas said nothing, but Clover imagined him nodding and smiling, the same sun that still heated her bare wet sex glinting on his beautiful golden hair.

Strong hands, his hands, helped her climb off the table, and soon she was walking away from the group, perhaps even forgotten by them as they anticipated the arrival of the male slave.

God, what will they do to him? Clover thought. A sudden drop in temperature told her she was indoors, in some sort of cool and shady entrance hall.

Will they bring him off too? she mused, feeling her body rouse again, against the odds, at the thought of it, and even more strangely, at the thought of being his mistress.

CHAPTER

12

Contrary to what she'd been expecting, the room assigned to Clover was beautiful and luxurious. She'd anticipated a little box at best, and possibly even a cell, perhaps below ground, but her accommodation would have graced a five-star hotel.

After escorting her upstairs, Lukas had left her alone, and she was grateful. She needed time to herself, not only to attend to her personal ablutions, but to think. She had to fully absorb her impressions of what had happened to her so far, and to speculate on what lay ahead.

During a long, cool shower, complete with an array of designer toiletries ranging from richly lathering super-fatted soap to a hair conditioner she knew for certain was exclusive to a top London salon, Clover found herself exploring the portion of her body so recently laid open to all and sundry. As she soaped and rinsed her pussy, she quickly found herself roused again, as much from the memories as from the friction of the soft and fluffy body-mop.

You liked it, didn't you? she accused herself, delicately manipulating her clitoris. She imagined herself on that table again, and felt her flesh leap at the thought of strange, greedy fingers pulling and poking, and pushing inside her. She wanted to be back there again, or on a different table, her legs drawn wide open – shackled perhaps? – while a succession of men, and women, fingered and tested her.

'Oh God,' she groaned, clinging to the shower fittings while she climaxed heavily, her other hand clamped between her legs.

Later, emerging from her en suite bathroom, her face and body creamed and pampered, her hair still a little damp, it came as no surprise to find that her clothes had been removed and no replacements left. When she went to the door, she found it locked. Not only were her suit, shoes and stockings gone, but there was a covered tray sitting on the delicate antique side table by the window. When she lifted the cloth, she found a delicious light meal of chicken in a creamy sauce with tiny vegetables, complete with a large glass of wine that proved to be equally exquisite.

Starving, she attacked the food, deriving an added enjoyment in sitting completely naked to eat it. The room was warm, and it seemed only natural to dispense with the thick, towelling bathrobe she'd been wearing.

Her window looked out over the side of the house, and lush green parkland dotted with mature trees. A few plump, strangely well-groomed sheep were grazing in the distance, and from the front of the house, she heard the faint drift of voices, talking and laughing.

When the volume rose suddenly and even from this distance she could detect a raised level of excitement, she wondered if the male slave had arrived and if they were putting him to the same kind of tests she'd endured. She imagined him bare from the waist down, ejaculating copiously as someone casually pumped his shaft, and she felt an overpowering urge to touch herself again.

Glancing down at her food, she suddenly felt like laughing. How rude was it to masturbate while you were eating? Was it on a level with playing with yourself in church or perhaps behind a chair when your grandparents were in the room? But the image of the unknown man being abused and tormented excited her intensely, so she slid a hand between her legs and rubbed herself until she climaxed. Then she finished her food and her wine, grinning and feeling extraordinarily pleased with herself.

By this time, the sounds from the distant patio had died away entirely, and, judging by the now setting sun, she guessed that people had left to change for dinner. She'd had her dinner, and her orgasm, but she still felt aroused and uneasy. Leaving her tray, she prowled the room, looking in drawers and wardrobes for any sign of clothing. There was nothing, and realising that, she felt her body rousing again. She was nude and helpless, and pretty soon they would come for her. When moisture began to trickle down her thighs yet again, she rushed to the bathroom and washed herself, but that led only to more masturbation and another frustratingly inconclusive climax.

As darkness fell, she lay on the bed without switching on the light. Now and again, she fingered herself lightly, but she felt too distracted and wound up to bother with more than that.

A nap would be nice, she thought, although she accepted it was unlikely she would actually fall asleep. But against all the odds, a short while later she drifted off.

She awoke to find that she had her hand jammed between her legs again. And that Lukas was standing beside the bed, looking down at her.

The sight of him made her want to leave her hand where it was.

He looked amazing. His tight leather trousers clung daringly to the shape of his thighs and his genitalia, but from the waist up, he was naked, his torso gleaming. His musculature was astonishing. Developed but not massive; beautifully cut, yet not grotesque. His bare chest was hairless, and his lean abdomen sported the classic six-pack definition. In addition to his leather jeans, he wore glassily polished jackboots and the heavily buckled belt with which Clover was rapidly becoming familiar.

His blue eyes flicked down to her crotch. 'You'll be punished for that,' he said. She snatched her fingers away, and when she tried to wipe the moisture down her thigh he caught her hand.

'You're a filthy little slut, aren't you, slave?' he continued, then, astonishingly, he enveloped her forefinger and middle finger in his mouth and savoured her essence. For a few seconds, Clover felt the heat and caress of his tongue, then he let her go, dashing her hand away quite forcefully.

'Wh-what happens now?' she stammered, looking at his calm, beautiful face.

'Don't speak unless you're given leave to,' he said, reaching for a large, flat white cardboard box, which Clover noticed for the first time on the end of the bed. Her lips moved, as if driven by the dozens of questions she was no longer allowed to articulate.

Inside the box, swathed in tissue, were a number of items. The first of which Lukas drew out, while motioning for Clover to stand.

What he held up before her was a corset, or perhaps, more accurately, a basque or waist-cincher. It was fashioned from a most exquisite black taffeta, with a subtle bronze sheen. Black piping trimmed the edges and delineated the series of long bones that gave it its shape. Satin-bound laces hung from the back, and, as far as Clover could see, it had no bra cups and would reach no further down than her belly button.

'Hold it against you while I fasten it,' instructed Lukas, handing her the garment.

Clover obeyed, her suspicions confirmed. The cups were no more than a sixteenth, just bands that cradled the undersides of her breasts, which were pushed up to vulgar prominence by the underwiring. Below, her entire belly, groin and buttocks were left bare.

'Stand straight,' ordered Lukas quietly, setting to work with the hooks and eyes, and then the lacing.

Almost immediately, Clover gasped at the grip of the thing. Just hooked, it clung to her like a second skin, embracing her rib cage, but a moment later, after some deft handling from Lukas, she felt it begin to tighten even more. He'd swiftly inserted the laces and was beginning to cinch her in.

'Breathe in.'

Tighter and tighter. Clover felt a real panic building

up inside her, as well as the physical sensations. Remorselessly, the boned bodice began to close in on her, restructuring her.

'Hold on to the bed-post.'

Feeling light-headed, Clover obeyed him, and then to her alarm, felt the pressure of Lukas's booted foot in the small of her back. He was using it as leverage to tighten the corset even more.

'Oh God,' she gasped, aware of her disobedience, but unable to contain herself. The corset held in her waist like a steel embrace and forced all her internal organs downwards, creating alarming pressure low in her belly. The weight of her vitals was bearing down on her sex from within, stimulating the root of her clitoris and even the sensitive nerve endings that lined her rectum and her anus. In helpless response, her vagina fluttered and her traitorous juices began to ooze slowly out of her.

Lukas tested her, slipping his tapered fingers lightly into her channel, and with no possible way to control herself, she experienced an instantaneous mini orgasm. She cried out as her clit leapt and danced.

He didn't tell her she'd be punished even more for that, but he didn't need to.

While she panted, and tried to catch her constrained breath, Lukas removed more things from the box.

First, a narrow, black leather collar with a silver d-ring, which he buckled around her neck as if she were a dog. Then, a pair of black patent court shoes with higher heels than she'd ever worn before. She swayed precariously when he made her step into them.

'Let's see you, then,' he said softly, stepping away from her. 'Do a twirl.'

Clover complied, tottering on the heels and gasping at the way even the slightest movement of her corseted body seemed to stimulate her. She managed the turn without disgracing herself, then felt a sudden surge of happy confidence.

Glancing down at Lukas's groin revealed that he had a massive hard-on.

You can't control yourself either, she thought with some elation, wondering what it would be like to be fucked while wearing this abominable constriction.

'Good,' he said, his face still impassive, but his eyes laughing. For just a split second he reached down and cupped himself, and Clover imagined she might have seen him give her the faintest nod of acknowledgement.

Then it was all business again and he was taking more items from the white cardboard box and laying them out on the bed.

The ubiquitous handcuffs. A dog leash to go with her dog's collar. A domino eye-mask made of soft, black leather, such as might be worn by a bandit or a reveller at the Venetian Carnival.

The first two, unsurprisingly, were for Clover, and Lukas snapped her hands behind her back in the cuffs, and attached the leash to her collar. But the last item, the mask, he fastened around his own eyes; the dark leather making his blue eyes look dangerous and even more dazzling. It should have seemed silly to see him done up like the Lone Ranger awaiting his Tonto, but instead, he looked mysterious, almost magical. Silently, she hoped that some time during the course of this interlude, he might make love to her while he was wearing the domino.

'Come along now,' he urged, tugging lightly on the leash, 'your audience awaits and they don't take kindly to tardiness.'

I'll bet they don't take kindly to anything, thought Clover as she trotted behind him along the corridor. The heels were difficult to walk in, and the compression on her belly was a constant tormenting stimulation, but at least Lukas seemed not to want to tug her along ignominiously. He let her find her own pace and the leash remained slack, and when they descended the broad sweeping staircase, he took her arm to support her.

When they reached a pair of massive double doors that opened off the imposing hall, he was less kind, however. He adjusted her breasts quite roughly in the minuscule cups of the basque, and pinched her nipples hard to bring them to an even stiffer state of erection. Then, completely without warning, he kissed her brutally hard on the mouth, nipping at her lower lip and making it swell slightly and redden. As he exerted one last moment of crushing pressure with his lips, he twisted her nipples again, so forcefully that tears sprang into her eyes.

She wanted to rage at him, demand why he was suddenly being such a brute, but she knew his purpose. It was part of the presentation. She had to look moist-eyed, pouty-lipped, ready and wanton. And, thorough in all things, Lukas had his own particular methods of preparation.

The room beyond was laid out in the way Clover imagined a Roman orgy might have been. Francis's guests – many of them masked as Lukas was – were lounging around in a circle on a collection of couches, easy chairs and chaise longues. The lighting in the perimeter of the room was subdued, provided by wall lanterns and several table lamps, but focused spotlights dramatically illuminated the central area.

And from some unseen fixture attached to the high, moulded ceiling, a glistening chain dangled into the circles of overlapping light.

A familiar voice rang out.

'Ah! Excellent, the first item of our evening's entertainment has arrived.' Francis Black's voice sounded expansive and genuinely happy. 'And my congratulations to you, Lukas, she's beautifully prepared, as always.'

Clover glanced sideways to see her golden captor nod in acknowledgement.

How many other women had he brought to gatherings like this to toy with?

But before she had chance to brood, Francis was speaking again.

'Let's get on with this. I'm eager to see her tested and I'm sure everybody else is.'

Lukas led Clover forward and in a quick deft action, he removed the leash from her collar, then clipped the dangling ceiling chain to the cuffs at her wrists. Somehow, she'd formed the impression that the cuffs would be unfastened and refastened so that her hands were drawn over her head, but instead, the connection was made with her hands still behind her. There was a whirr of hidden machinery, the chain begin to shorten and suddenly she saw the configuration's diabolical purpose.

As her hands came up behind her, she was tipped forwards, her head and breasts dangling down and her thighs and bottom pushed out and lifted into vulgar prominence. To keep her footing, she had to part her legs and show her sex.

She was a perfect, vulnerable target for a beating. Or a fucking. Or even worse.

Looking through her own spread thighs, Clover could seen Lukas's long, leather-clad legs and booted feet behind her. Someone handed him something, and a second later, she saw him whisk what looked like a long-handled riding whip through the air. Involuntarily, she moaned, unable to imagine the degree of pain such a thing could inflict, but knowing it would be grievous.

'I think our young friend would probably feel more comfortable with a gag, don't you?' Francis seemed to aim his comment at the watchers in general, but from one of the couches a man rose and came towards Clover's dangling form.

Taking her by the head, the newcomer thrust a round rubber ball into her mouth, and then quickly fastened it in place with straps. It felt chokingly enormous, and Clover immediately began to salivate. She felt like weeping when her drool trickled out from around the obstruction and began to dribble down her chin.

Wimp! Don't give in! You've got to be impressive, she told herself, swaying on the chain and cataloguing the multitude of twinges and discomforts she already felt, even before that long whip had come anywhere near her. Her shoulders ached from the unnatural position. Her belly felt as if it were about to burst. Even her jaw felt as if it were dislocating around the rubber ball.

Glancing upside down around the room, she saw people laughing and talking and pointing to her. The conversations were low, but she knew they were discussing and evaluating her near-naked body and her stance. Unconsciously, she arched her back, offering her bottom and sex more readily. Between her legs, she saw Lukas stop prowling, stop swishing. He too took up his position, his long booted legs slightly braced . . .

'When you're ready, Lukas,' said Francis Black casually.

But what about me? Clover thought.

Even as the words formed in her brain, she registered a whistling sound cutting the air, and felt herself knocked forward on her chain, half stumbling.

She started to think, It's not too bad, I can't feel anything, then a bolt of white sensation, so huge and breathtaking that it eclipsed the simple word 'pain', scored across the crown of her buttocks and the inside of her head echoed with the deafening sound of the scream she could not utter.

Oh God, no! I can't do this! she wailed like a wounded animal inside her mind. I can't! I can't!

But the pain came again, and then again, each time setting her spinning and stumbling on the chain, her brain a blank turmoil and the flesh of her bottom in another world of torment. Dimly, she was aware of Lukas on the prowl again, following her momentum so that he always hit her in the place that hurt the most.

A voice entered the chaotic mix.

'Ah, the first six. Well done, my dears. Let's take a short break, shall we?'

Only six? It felt like hours of beating and hundreds of blows. Clover was struggling to stop her inner screaming. She could hear another noise now too, and, to her horror, she realised it was herself. Muffled by the gag, she was making uncouth, wet, grunting and gobbling sounds. She tried to stop herself, but couldn't. There seemed no other way to express the burning agony that was raging in her buttocks.

Tears streamed from her eyes, blurring her vision, and, against all reason, she felt a hot, slippery stream of lubrication, sliding out of her exposed pussy. She could actually feel a couple of trickles running down the inside of her thighs as far as her knees.

Oh God, had she wet herself? Her nerve ends were so confused that she simply couldn't tell.

Fingers touched her bottom and she shouted into the gag. She could tell it was Lukas, but he wasn't being kind. He probed firmly along the lines of pain, then pushed his forefinger rudely into her vagina. It came away dripping and he casually wiped the juice across the site of her injury, making her gulp and moan again. Her eyes nearly started out of her head when he began to exert pressure on her anus.

'You're quite right, dear boy.' Francis's voice seemed to drift on the sea of sensations. 'It needs something there, doesn't it? Let's attend to that.'

Two women from the group rose and approached Clover, and Francis spoke again. 'Show the slave the amusements,' he instructed.

One woman caught Clover by the hair and made her lift her head, while the other held out two objects in front of her.

Oh no!

One was a cloudy glass sphere with a twisted white cord hanging from it, adorned with a tassel. The other was a small vial of some viscous liquid, possibly oil.

Oh no! Oh no! cried Clover inside, as the two women moved around behind her, and almost immediately she felt their unkind hands upon her, stirring up her torment. One of them pulled apart her buttocks in a swift, businesslike way, while the other tipped the oil into her cleft. Then, while she was still being held open, she felt the pressure of the glass sphere being pushed against the rim of her nether opening.

It's too big! It's too big! she wanted to scream at them. But they kept pushing, opening her remorselessly, making space where there shouldn't be any. Just when she thought she was going to split open, the glass ball popped inside her ... and then another even more loathsome and shaming sensation gripped her bowels.

An intense urge to evacuate.

She gobbled behind her gag again, clenching her buttocks and dancing on her chain, fighting the horrible, horrible urges in her flesh. Then she heard a voice, soft and familiar, in her ear.

'Stay calm ... It's not going to happen.' A hand brushed against her dangling hair, smoothing it from her brow. 'Believe me. I've been there.'

Lukas. Lukas had felt this disgusting feeling. And he'd survived.

Miraculously, the worst of the sensation that she might soil herself disappeared almost immediately. Only to be replaced by a dark and voluptuous stimulation that even made its presence felt through the burning in her buttocks. The ball rocked inside her, tantalising sensitive nerve receptors that had never been piqued before. The juice dribbling down her thighs thickened and her clitoris leapt and seemed to swell.

Oh, please touch me! she begged silently, new tears of pure amazement sliding down her cheeks. She'd been made to suffer the most extreme pain she could imagine, and now been abused in the most abominable and intrusive way, but all she could think about was coming! She rocked and jiggled her body, trying to get some ease for her clit. She didn't care what the assembled audience thought of her; dear God, she bloody well *wanted* them to know that she was turned on! *And* that she was every bit the horny, depraved pervert they all were . . . perhaps even more so!

Unspeakably lewd images began to parade themselves through Clover's mind, and some were so grotesque that when Lukas began to beat her again, she was almost glad of the pain. If she could think such things, she deserved the extremes of agony . . .

But with every burning blow that fell, her arousal spiralled. The fire in her buttocks was like a ribbon that wound itself around the glass sphere, and around her clit, ever tightening and bringing her closer and closer to climax.

So lost was she in the kiss of the whip, and in her own mounting arousal, that it took her a few seconds to realise that the blows had suddenly ceased. Her bottom hurt so much now that it was hard to tell where individual pains began and ended. She swayed on the chain, looked between her legs and saw that the whip was on the floor and Lukas was advancing towards her with his long, elegant stride.

Coming around to the front, he reached down and raised her head, making her crane her neck to look at him. His eyes were like blue jewels behind the menacing black mask, and when she let her glance go lower, she saw his erection was bigger than ever, the long, hard line of his cock clearly outlined beneath the fine leather of his trousers. Before her astonished eyes, he unfastened his heavy leather belt and unzipped himself, taking out his swollen penis and rubbing it against her cheeks.

Oh God, take this gag out, she begged him silently, longing for a taste of him, and, almost as if he'd heard the plea, he reached behind her head and unbuckled the hateful straps. Easing the rubber ball from her mouth he flung it away across the room. Answering her prayers, he thrust his cock summarily between her lips, then took hold of her head to push himself deeper and chokingly deeper, to the back of her throat.

Clover closed her eyes and concentrated on not gagging and simply adoring the sensation of her mouth completely stuffed with his flesh. He was taking her roughly, jamming himself in with little tenderness and finesse, but she gloried in that. Use me, she begged him, use me like a thing. Take your pleasure in me, I *am* your slave. I'll suffer *anything* . . .

Again, she experienced the bizarre sensation that he might have read her mind. He stilled, his penis deep, almost making her choke, and, for a moment, she felt his hand glide gently over her hair. A second later, he was withdrawing and a trail of saliva trickled shamingly down Clover's chin.

But you haven't come, she thought, her brain whirling as she wondered what was going on. However, when Lukas walked around behind her and tugged on the string attached to the glass sphere inside her rectum, she read *his* mind, and moaned at the thought of what was coming next.

The woman who'd oiled her before stepped forward again, and Clover felt the sticky fluid trickling into her bottom crack, as Lukas exerted a firm pull on the cord and the sphere came popping out of her. Clover gasped as her anus seemed to gape hugely and the continued flow of oil seeped inside her, smoothing the way for what she feared, but also longed for. Something hard and warm and silky pressed itself against her nether entrance, gently at first, then with increasing determination. Her body protested, and tried to close up, but there was no quarter given and the penetration continued.

'Oh God!' she squealed, as the muscular ring yielded and Lukas's penis slid home inside her bottom.

Again came the horrific sensation as her bowel tried to expel him, but he held her firm, his thumbs gouging into her punished buttocks, and as she howled again, her innards ceased to protest and accepted the intruder in her dark and secret entrance.

As Lukas slowly started to thrust, the sensation overload in her backside and innards seemed to change in quality. The agony of her beaten flesh metamorphosed into a high, almost silvery pleasure, and the head of Lukas's cock inside her seemed to jostle against a million sensitive nerve endings, each one of them connected directly to her clitoris. It was overwhelming, and infernal, and, at last, and with a long, shaking, animal groan that she barely recognised as her own, Clover began to come.

Huge, wrenching spasms ripped through her sex and her bottom, clamping down on, and embracing the cock lodged inside her. Clover saw red mist, felt herself transported to another world, then came back right into the real one, her ecstasy soaring, when Lukas jerked inside her, shouted out a profanity, and began to climax.

CHAPTER

13

Clover held in a moan as she slumped back against the wall she was chained to. The plasterwork was hard, and even though Lukas had rubbed some soothing salve into the marks from her whipping, any contact with her bottom was sharply painful. But she felt exhausted and had to take some kind of rest.

Once the glorious ignominy of her sodomy was over, she'd been let down and allowed to rest a few moments, lying on the carpet, but all too soon she had to make way for the next item in the 'floorshow'. Lukas drew her to her feet, not unkindly, then gave her a long drink of water and led her over to an area of the wall just behind a vacant armchair. Here he unfastened her cuffs, refastened them so her hands were in front of her, then fastened her up to a sturdy hook above her head. She was positioned facing into the room, presumably so she could see the show, and, after kissing her once on the lips, Lukas had replaced the hateful ball-gag in her mouth.

The glass sphere had been replaced inside her, but it still felt like Lukas's magnificent penis stretching and distending her fundament. It was hard to believe the pleasure those sensations had given her, or the strength of the orgasms, but she had to accept now that almost everything that was dark and perverted turned her on.

She watched Lukas take a sip from his drink, heard him murmur something to the woman sitting next to him, making her laugh, but she sensed he was very much aware of her behind him, and even though he appeared to be ignoring her as a worthless slave, used and discarded, they were still very much in contact with one another.

As she hung there, wishing he'd allow her to kneel on the floor at his feet and kiss his shiny boots, a small commotion across the room drew her attention to the doorway.

The next 'item' had arrived and three familiar figures had just entered the room.

If Clover could have spoken, she would have exclaimed, Bloody hell! As it was, she smiled to herself the best she could at the sight of the three newcomers, a man and two women.

So that's where Olivia's been, she thought, admiring her erstwhile benefactress and the way the older woman's voluptuous figure was crammed into a tight bodysuit of dark red vinyl. Olivia's lush breasts were threatening to spill out of the suit's extremely minimal bra cups, and it was cut so high and had such a narrow crotch strip that Clover could see now why the other woman shaved her pussy so stringently. She too wore a black domino mask like Lukas's, and her luxuriant hair tumbled sexily down her back.

Her female companion was the dark and dramatic Circe, and wearing a very similar outfit of midnight blue with silver piping. The Hispanic woman had longer legs, and a much slimmer waist, and her black hair hung in a shimmering sheet all the way down to her barely covered bottom, but her breasts, though beautiful, could in no way compete with Olivia's.

The man standing between them, naked and eyes downcast, was the biggest surprise.

Nathan Ribiero, whom Clover had last seen lording it over a crying girl at Francis Black's party, and whipping her bottom with ruthless gusto.

Nathan's a slave now, she thought, feeling not only a sense of surprise, but also a new surge of lust in her belly. A naked male slave. Were they going to whip him and torment him for their entertainment too?

But it looked to Clover as if some of the tormenting had already begun. Nathan's large dark eyes were wet and he looked as if he'd been weeping. And more interestingly, someone – presumably Olivia and Circe – had been doing something diabolical to his cock.

Nathan was hugely erect, his penis so stiff and red that it looked quite sore, and there were what appeared to be a series of leather straps around it and his scrotum. He was bound tight, forced to stay shamingly hard until someone freed him and granted him relief.

Feeling her own sex flutter, Clover wondered how long he'd been kept stiff like that, and just how much longer his two mistresses intended him to stay that way.

'Ah, Nathan my boy,' said Francis Black cheerfully as

the sorry young man was led forward into the centre of the circle, just as Clover had been.

'Are you ready to entertain us?' the older man enquired, letting a bystander, an elegant young man with short dark hair and pretty, rather pointed features, light him a cigarette. 'You'll have to go a long way to beat the show we've just seen.' He gave a slight acknowledging nod in Clover's direction.

Clover lowered her gaze respectfully, but couldn't help feeling a little pleased. She didn't much care if Nathan did excel her, just so long as she was allowed to remain here to see it happen.

But if she did, she was going to get excited again, even more aroused than she already was. And then how would she be able to ease the ache between her legs? She was fastened up, and it was quite difficult to move. She supposed she could try squeezing her legs together and clenching herself inside, around the glass sphere, but suddenly she wasn't so sure she wanted to do that. The drink of water Lukas had given her had been long and cold and it had already passed through her and settled heavily in her bladder. It was starting to feel uncomfortable, and much more than normal due to the presence of the glassy obstruction in her bottom. Surreptitiously, she lifted a leg and pressed one thigh across the other in an attempt to ease the situation.

As if he'd heard her uneasy movement, Lukas turned in his seat and gave her a long, questioning look. Reaching across the back of his armchair, he laid his fingers lightly over the curve of her belly, then pressed down, low, just above her crotch.

You bastard! You know! You gave me that water on purpose! She moaned behind her gag, as his fingers probed her discomfort. Then, with a soft laugh, he rose from his seat and came to stand beside her, gesturing to a maid for a bottle of water from the sideboard as he did so.

No! begged Clover silently, realising that the attention of the group had moved from Nathan's plight to her own. But Lukas only smiled and slid his fingers around behind the back of her head, removing her gag.

'Oh no, please,' she whispered to him, as he took the bottle from the maid, uncapped it, and held it firmly to her lips.

'Oh yes,' he said, his voice gentle, almost sweet. 'For me, you must.'

Tears trickled from Clover's eyes as she began to drink, the chilled water sliding down her throat and seeming almost immediately to add to the horrible pressure in her bladder. Lukas kept the bottle at her mouth for several long moments, forcing her to drink at least a couple of pints, and by the time he took it away, she was crying freely and in great distress.

With exquisite tenderness he wiped her tears, then kissed her on the lips. It should have felt so beautiful, but the discomfort down below meant she couldn't enjoy it. She gasped against his mouth as he caressed her belly, his fingers tormenting.

'Be quiet now,' he said as he drew away from her, and after one last peck on the cheek, he pressed the gag back into her mouth.

I can't bear this, thought Clover, her body wracked with a new and shameful form of torture. She felt sweat break out all over her skin as the weight of her waters seemed to sink down and press hard on the root of her clitoris, turning her on even more. She could feel fluid sliding down her legs again. Not urine yet, but the juices of her arousal flowing copiously like a river of shame down her legs. She could even smell it, hot and pungent, rising around her.

Through the veil of her own suffering, she watched Nathan being strung up, his arms pulled tight above his head, his fettered penis dancing as he moved. Olivia moved forward and began to play with him, squeezing and flicking at his cock, while Circe selected an evil-looking switch from amongst a selection of implements.

Nathan struggled on his chain and begged, 'Please! No!' He was ungagged, and it seemed that he was going to be allowed to scream and yell and plead for mercy. For a moment, Clover felt rebellious. Why had she had her mouth stoppered and not Nathan? But then she saw that perhaps the gag was a form of solace. At least she hadn't been able to embarrass herself by being totally pathetic. In the state she was in now, she was glad of it.

'Try to contain yourself, slave,' said Olivia imperiously, her fingers still moving unceasingly on Nathan's penis. He bit his lip, and appeared to make a supreme effort, but his eyes were huge and swimming, like a whipped puppy dog, even before the beating had begun.

By now, Circe was testing the whip, just as Lukas had done before her, but with a nod to Olivia, she now raised it in readiness. Olivia took hold of Nathan's penis and nodded back at her exotic friend.

Nathan screeched at the top of his voice when the blow fell, then jerked and danced, held in place only by Olivia's grip on his manhood. Circe struck again and the whole process was repeated. Then again, and again, and again.

When Nathan wasn't bellowing, Clover tried to listen to the murmurs of comment that were going around the circle. She sensed disapproval. The group weren't all that impressed with Nathan, and she felt a tiny glow of something like satisfaction that her own performance had been infinitely superior. Which was some comfort psychologically, but didn't help with the bursting fullness in her bladder.

If only I could touch my clit, I might feel better, she thought, glancing down at her sweat-slicked body and the bulge of her abdomen pressing out from beneath the edge of her corset. Once again, she tried to discreetly shift her thighs in an attempt to give herself some ease, but the slight movement only agitated the sensation of a swelling ball of lead bearing down inside her.

Oh God, I'm going to wet myself, she thought, I know I am. Any moment now, the pee is going to start cascading down my legs.

Once again Lukas turned to her as if sensing a new crisis in her torments.

'Does this excite you?' he said softly, his long hand settling lightly on her swollen, pushed-out belly as he nodded towards the writhing, shouting Nathan. 'Would you like to be the one hitting him?' The tip of his finger slid into her wet cleft, but cruelly avoided the protruding bead of her clitoris.

Please, please, touch me! she screamed silently, but from somewhere found the presence of mind to simply nod in answer to Lukas's enquiry. She *did* want to beat Nathan. She wanted to thrash him within an inch of his life. Make him suffer for what was happening to her now. Make him a surrogate, because she could never take her frustration out on Lukas.

Or could she? Could she string *him* up and whip him? Torment him with pain and butt plugs and a hard, swollen bladder? She groaned into her gag as the newly forming images only ramped up her arousal.

'I think you need to be out of here, don't you?' Lukas said, withdrawing his hand from her sex and looking her in the eye.

Clover nodded furiously, and, in response, he reached up and unfastened her cuffs from the hook. Turning, he sought the eyes of Francis Black, who nodded, as if giving Lukas permission to withdraw from the entertainment.

Walking was horrendously difficult. Clover could hardly bear even the slightest movement that jostled her bladder, and the high-heeled shoes created a dangerous instability. She gasped with every step, convinced that, at any moment, she'd embarrass herself, but somehow they got to the door without incident, or even attracting much attention. As she left the room, following Lukas on her leash, she risked a quick look back and felt a rush of heat at the sight that they were leaving.

Nathan was still moaning and sobbing, but the beating had temporarily been halted. He was standing up on his toes, trying to grab at the chain and get away from a new torment . . .

Circe had thrust the handle of her whip into his anus.

On the way to her room, Lukas halted Clover a couple of times just to touch her and caress the drum-tight skin of her lower belly. Each time, Clover cried piteously, and he kissed her lips gently where they were stretched around the gag. By the time they reached their destination, she was almost fainting.

But a new trial awaited her, she soon realised. Instead

of escorting her straight to the bathroom, where she was quite prepared, even longing to squat on the toilet and urinate in front of him, Lukas led her to the bed instead, and made her lie down upon it and on a rubber sheet that some thoughtful maid had spread across the luxurious counterpane.

Oh, please, no! she implored him with her eyes as he secured her, on her back, to the bed-head, unfastening her from the cuffs and attaching each hand separately behind her head, using soft, padded cords. To her ankles he attached a new set of cuffs, each one on the end of a pole so that her legs were widely spread apart. The position stirred fresh heat in her punished buttocks, but Clover only began to moan and gobble behind her gag when he took a fresh bottle of frostily chilled water from the bedside table.

'I can't . . . I can't . . .' she gasped, when he took the gag from her mouth and supported her head to make her drink.

'Please? For me?' he coaxed, kissing her lips before holding the bottle to them. 'It gives me a delicious turn-on to know that you're dying to piss, that you're in torment with a bursting bladder. Please, drink, for me.' Against her bare hip, she felt the pressure of his hard-on.

Weeping freely, Clover drank, feeling an instant increase in the infernal sensations. Sweat broke out afresh all over her body, and she longed to be able to close her tethered thighs. Her clitoris felt as if it were standing out on a stalk.

She could manage no more than a quarter of the bottle, and Lukas didn't insist she drink any more. Instead, he wiped her brow with tenderness, then kissed her, just once, on the lips.

'I'm going to leave you now for a while,' he said rising from the bed, and making Clover pant when the mattress rocked, 'but I'll be thinking of you all the time, imagining what you're feeling, my pretty girl.' He paused and glanced down at her taut belly. 'Hell, I've been there, I know what it's like.' He reached out and stroked his fingertip over her clit, and Clover sobbed. 'Not that, of course, but something like it.' With the same hand he cupped the enormous bulge of his erection through the leather of his trousers, then with one last, long, burning look at her, her strode away from the bed and left. Clover heard the click of the door being locked behind him.

Oh God, oh God, oh God, what if I wet myself? she thought, as the hideous pressure of her waters seemed to gather and intensify with her helplessness. The need to pee now was agony, but at the same time a sexual stimulation it was impossible to ignore. She felt as if she were in the grip of some potent hallucinogen that paraded lewd images in front of her, fantasies that only increased the tumescence in her sex and in her clitoris.

No! she told herself, as her fevered mind imagined drinking yet more water, while Lukas pummelled her belly and pushed even greater obstructions into her beleaguered body. Massive vibrators buzzed in her vagina and her anus; greedy, lustful hands plucked at her nipples, fingered her between her legs and between her buttocks; her mouth was filled with someone's cock; she was forced to drink more water, then to felate another man . . . Her pussy pulsated helplessly and she felt moisture between her legs, but she didn't know whether it was her body leaking or just the silky honey of her arousal.

195

For a long time, she seemed to float on a sea of pure torment, the whole of her consciousness focused on the dreadful sensations in her distended bladder. 'I can't, I can't, I can't,' she chanted to herself, wishing she could just relax and let her flow come, but inhibited by the perverse desire to hold it in because her distress was pleasing to Lukas.

Eventually, when she was babbling deliriously and unable to stop herself trembling, no matter how much it hurt, the door opened and Lukas walked towards the bed, completely naked and stunningly erect.

'My darling,' he murmured, kissing her lips and touching her breasts. Clover moaned beneath his mouth and prayed and prayed that he would either touch her between her legs . . . or *not* touch her between her legs. But instead, working quickly, he unfastened her hands and freed her from the spreader bar, then drew her up from the bed and helped her towards the bathroom, his arms around her waist. Once they were there, he lifted her out of her shoes, then unfastened her corset, cutting the laces to get it off faster. The last thing he removed was the leather collar from around her neck, before bundling her unceremoniously into the luxurious double shower.

Clover whimpered and cried at the jags of sensation his actions caused, then half screamed as he set the shower running . . .

It was too much! Her bladder couldn't take the teeming of the water and she began to urinate, but even as the flow started, Lukas lifted her effortlessly, parted her legs, and brought her opened sex down on his jutting erection.

'Oh God! Oh God!' Clover shrieked, convulsing in an immediate, gigantic orgasm, her loins jerking and clenching in agonising pleasure, as her waters gushed out of her and streamed down her legs and his. For a few seconds, she blacked out, then came to again, still climaxing and urinating, the blinding spasms all the more breathtaking because deep inside her they were contracting around the glass sphere still buried in her rectum.

Lukas held her tight, his broad chest heaving as his hips worked against hers and his own orgasm began. He shouted several oaths in her ear, then buried his face in her neck as she felt his semen leap inside her.

CHAPTER

14

The days that followed had the quality of a dream for Clover. But she supposed that was the essence of the secret world. There was nothing about it that was like normal life at all.

After their passionate coming together in the shower, Lukas had cleaned Clover up and put her back to bed. He'd fastened her hands above her head to the bedhead again, but this time quite loosely so she was able to find a comfortable position. Even tied up, it felt like paradise compared to the torments that had gone before.

Then, to her enormous surprise, he'd stripped off and got into bed beside her, his hands running swiftly over her body before he settled down for sleep. A few moments later, he was breathing evenly and dead to the world.

For Clover, it had taken longer to settle. Not because of the bondage. In fact, oddly enough, that felt natural.

No, it was the presence of this man in the bed at her side. In the moonlight, he'd looked like a slumbering angel, and she'd found it hard to believe the devilish mind that lay beyond those closed eyes and that crown of white-gold. What he'd done to her earlier with the water had been a truly fiendish exercise in erotic control and dominance, yet as he slept, he looked as innocent as a virgin choirboy.

Eventually she had slept, only to be wakened twice in the night by Lukas parting her thighs to take her. The second time, having made sure she'd had a couple of orgasms with him inside her, he'd withdrawn, straddled her face and come in her mouth.

As she'd drifted back to sleep again, she'd thought dreamily, I'll do absolutely anything for this man.

The next morning began a series of bizarre and sensual interludes. Tests and trials that Clover relished, not in spite of but *because* they made her feel vulnerable and used. Everything about them was designed to expose her, both physically and emotionally, and to yield up her every reaction and response for the entertainment of the group assembled at Francis Black's beautiful house. Lukas was her keeper and her mentor. He expedited these displays and was constantly at her side.

He led her as she was paraded naked for the scrutiny of the others. He arranged her in extreme positions, prepared her body for outrage after outrage, slid dildoes and vibrators into her orifices and smeared her genitalia with aphrodisiac potions so that she writhed lewdly in her bondage in a futile attempt to get even the smallest bit of ease.

And, of course, it was almost always Lukas who

whipped her. Others sometimes took a turn, but he was the one who truly mastered her, with whips or paddles, his lethal belt, or just his hand.

Before too long, Clover's bottom was almost always pink, as were the fronts and backs of her thighs. Yet strangely, once the punishment itself was over, real pain didn't seem to linger long. Lukas's gentle and repeated applications of cooling salve seemed to mellow any hurts she received into just a warm glow that was more a turn-on than a discomfort.

With every hour and ordeal that passed, she adored him more.

Some trials stood out in her mind more than others. For instance, being stretched out on a table on her back, her legs spread wide and dangling over the edge, while Lukas whipped the tender insides of her thighs. This time she was allowed to cry, and she did so, wailing piteously with every stroke that fell. All the while, the assembled group chatted and laughed, eating a delicious lunch while Clover writhed, her dripping crotch on show.

On another occasion, after a hard beating on her bottom with a riding crop, Lukas bound her into an ingenious wooden punishment frame out on the patio, her legs raised and spread wide again. Drinks were being served in an impromptu cocktail party, and she was the divertissement for any of the male guests who were randy. All manner of sex games were taking place amongst the group, but those men who were partnerless and in need of relief took advantage of Clover.

Again and again, they came up to her, stood between her legs, unzipped and entered her. Some were quick and concerned only with their own pleasure, but others were slower and seemed to need to see her come too.

I'm just a receptacle, thought Clover dazedly, as perhaps the eighth or tenth man toiled away inside her, a convenient body to assuage their lust.

Yet as she turned her head to the side, unwilling to let the man who was fucking her see her pleasure, she felt uplifted by the presence of Lukas at her side. As she groaned and climaxed, he stroked her brow and kissed her cheek.

And at night he shared her bed. He always tied her up, but despite that, and the fact that he seemed to want her far more frequently than a normal man would, he was mostly tender and almost loving in the way he dealt with her. Half asleep and dazed with pleasure as she felt him thrusting inside her, she imagined she heard him whisper unimaginable endearments and promises to her.

Sometimes she saw Nathan being punished too, and every time that happened, she felt a piquant thrill of curiosity. What would it be like to be the one with the whip in her hand?

Lying in bondage one night, with Lukas's hand between her thighs, Clover heard a faint cry echo up from the garden. A man's voice whimpering softly, expressing torment.

'What do you think of that?' quizzed Lukas, doing something clever and almost impossible with fingers and thumb that made her climax immediately.

'Incredible,' gasped Clover when she could speak again.

Lukas laughed softly. 'Well, actually, I was talking about Nathan. I was wondering what you thought about him being punished. Does it turn you on?'

Clover saw no reason to prevaricate. 'Yes, it does. A lot. Maybe one day I'd like to be on the other end of all this,' she said, wishing her hands were free so she could fondle Lukas's marvellous erection as it pressed against her thigh. 'And I wouldn't mind giving Nathan a good walloping either. He still seems an arrogant sod, despite the fact he's supposed to be a slave.'

Lukas was silent for a few moments, and Clover wondered if she'd said too much and would have to suffer for it. But then he spoke again.

'That's good, Clover,' he murmured, rubbing himself slowly against her, 'because Francis has another test for you tomorrow. The final one. If you pass it you can be a regular member of the group.'

'What test?' Clover felt a sudden fear, greater than her fear of pain even, but excitement surged up inside her too.

'To be a real member of the group, you have to be able to walk both paths, Clover,' Lukas went on, pausing only to kiss her briefly on the lips. 'You have to be able to take and to give. Do you understand me?'

'Yes,' she said, moving against him, 'yes, I do. And I want to be able to do that. But I'm afraid I might not have the ability. I know it's not an easy thing to do properly.'

Lukas fell silent again, his penis seeming to harden even more against her.

Eventually he said, 'You could practise before you do it in front of the group.'

'What do you mean?' she whispered, knowing exactly what he was saying, but almost afraid to believe it.

'You could practise now. On me.'

'But you're my master,' she said, in awe.

'Yes, but I've been a slave in my time, and I can be one again.' He reached up above their heads and freed her hands, then drew her up into a sitting position with him. 'I give the power to you now, Clover,' he said quietly. 'The tables are turned. Do with me what you will.' Almost before the words were out of his lips, he climbed gracefully out of bed and knelt down, his head bowed.

What do I do now? thought Clover, panicking.

Something suddenly dawned on her. Of the two sides of the S/M equation, the dominant's job was more difficult: decisions to make, a complex and believable persona to create, the burden of maintaining absolute control of the slave. All the submissive had to do was give in and accept.

I can't do this, she thought, then found herself automatically squaring her shoulders, straightening up. She rose to her feet and looked down on the man kneeling before her. He was hers to command, this beautiful, accomplished sexual master. How could she let him down now by behaving like a wimp?

It was difficult to feel queen-like and imperious when naked, but she sensed it was far more about attitude than accoutrements, so she glanced around quickly, sizing up the situation.

'Get up, slave,' she said, keeping her voice low and even the way Lukas always did, 'then place yourself across the bed. Sideways on. I want a good view of your bottom.'

With all the smooth elegance of his supermodel deportment, Lukas stood up and complied silently with her commands. He was already erect, and she wondered whether that came from the true joy of submission, or just because he was enjoying the game. It didn't really matter, she supposed, as long as he acted the part believably. And if he didn't, he'd be sorry, she told herself silently, feeling a frisson of understanding and connection with her sudden new status.

Was that a little gasp, a sigh as he laid himself and his enormous hard-on against the counterpane?

'Silence,' she bade him softly, almost undone by the gorgeous sight of his tight male buttocks presented to her. She'd never seen a better arse in all her life, and she couldn't even begin to imagine one more perfect.

And he was taking a risk by submitting to her. She knew nothing about the craft of punishment, and Lukas's body was a very public one. If she marked him in the wrong place, he could lose a contract, and his livelihood might be jeopardised.

So, what to hit him with? He mostly smacked her by hand in the bedroom, and if there were implements available, she didn't know where they were stored – and it wouldn't look very mistress-like to have to hunt for them. Then her eyes fell on his fearsome belt, dangling from the loops of his leather trousers where they lay over a chair.

Can I manage that? she asked herself. She imagined a flexible strip of leather would be much harder to control than something rigid like a switch or a cane. But suddenly she knew that the belt was the thing for her. Master that and she could master anything. She had to try.

Unshipping the belt from its loops, she took hold of the buckle and wound some of its length around her right hand. She hefted it quickly, just to get the weight of it, then lifted it up and fingered its thickness. Taking a couple of steps back, she positioned herself where she thought would give her the best impact on that perfect bottom with a open-armed stroke.

Clover had always been good at sports like tennis and hockey, and she knew her hand-to-eye co-ordination was exceptional. This was the same principle; using an implement to hit a target. In addition, this target wasn't moving *and* it was bigger than a tennis or hockey ball.

'Raise your bottom. Present yourself properly,' she told Lukas quietly. He was in exactly the right position anyway, but it would do no harm to order him around a little to keep him in line. His muscular body flexed, and she saw a shudder pass across his sculpted face where it was pressed against the bedspread. His long lashes flicked down as he closed his eyes in abject submission.

Oh well, here goes . . .

To her great satisfaction, Clover's first blow connected with flukish accuracy right across the very crown of Lukas's left buttock. There was a ringing crack as leather met flesh and her victim cried out in pain, his usually husky male voice strangely high and feminine.

Clover felt a deep, deep thrill, and a keen clench of pleasure in her belly.

Oh God, I've made Lukas scream like a little girl! This is amazing!

She was pleased with the cleanly defined red mark on the cheek of his bottom. It was exactly where it should be. Right in the centre. The guide for all the other strokes to follow.

She continued, placing the strokes carefully and

finding a sharp, erotic delight in the rapid rubescence of Lukas's flesh and the real pain and emotion in his cries. He wriggled too, but only briefly, after each stroke. All the rest of the time he held his pose with great composure, even though Clover could see that there were tears squeezing out from beneath his eyelashes.

I can do this! Clover thought triumphantly after about half a dozen strokes. I can really do it! She suddenly felt gripped by a wicked desire to really let rip. To pummel that exquisite backside to a bruised, crimson pulp and make its owner howl and squirm and beg for mercy.

And yet she held back. Better to conserve such a great lust to punish for tomorrow, when she would have to put on a show. It would be so much fun, and she would be able to be so much more evil when she had that uppity little bastard Nathan beneath the lash. She was revelling in beating Lukas, but all of a sudden there were other things she wanted to do with him instead. As far as she could tell he hadn't ejaculated, so why should that fabulous erection go to waste?

'Get up now,' she said, letting the belt uncurl from around her fingers and drop to the carpet. Looking Lukas in his damp blue eyes, and loving that fact that his pretty face was almost as red as his bottom, she walked slowly up to the bed, then climbed on to it and spread her legs.

'Now, service me, slave,' she ordered, unable to stop herself from laughing as she pointed to her sticky, exposed crotch.

His glorious penis bouncing, Lukas leaped eagerly to obey her.

* * *

As she walked towards the double doors leading to the main salon, Clover felt her innards clench with apprehension and excitement.

Would she be able to carry this off? Did she look the part? Would the assembled group believe in her and not laugh her off as an amateur?

She paused at the entrance, smoothing her fingers down her ribs, flank and hip. God, this bloody contraption was just as tight as the slave corset she'd been forced to wear, although at least it was marginally less revealing. But only just.

'You look sensational,' said Lukas, from just behind her. He reached for her arm and turned her to face him, as if performing a final 'pre-flight' check. 'Believe me,' he went on, sliding his hand along the same path hers had just traversed. When he reached the edge of the vinyl fabric where it was cut dangerously high over her hips, he slid his fingers beneath it and gave it a swift tug to make the narrow crotch piece sit more snugly. Satisfied with that, he cupped his hand between her legs and gave her a gentle, almost friendly squeeze.

Clover supposed she really did look sensational. The one-piece black vinyl bodysuit clung like liquid to every curve and contour, leaving no possible intimate feature of her anatomy to the imagination. Her aroused nipples stood out proudly, pressing against the shiny fabric, and, between her legs, the division of her sex was blatantly defined, the detail possible because Lukas had carefully shaved away every last scrap of her pubic hair.

The suit was her only garment, but her accessories were impressive: high black heels, which, having worn them for several days now, she was able to walk in gracefully; a leather domino mask just like the one

Lukas was wearing; and a pair of leather wrist cuffs and matching collar, studded with diamonds.

'The collar of a mistress,' he'd murmured, fastening it around her throat while he was still inside her. Was it only fifteen minutes ago that he'd been fucking her passionately to psych her up for the coming performance? Pounding into her with energy and determination, but not kissing her so he wouldn't mar the perfect, dramatic make-up he'd applied to her face or dishevel the smooth chignon created with her freshly washed blond hair.

'I'm not sure I can do this,' she said, butterflies in her stomach.

'Believe me, lady, you can do it,' said Lukas, his blue eyes glittering behind his mask as he reached around, gripped his own bottom through his leather jeans and grimaced. Clover imagined the reddened flesh that lay beneath the tight garment, and instantly wanted to fuck him again. Perhaps on top, so she could ride his pain and make him scream . . .

'Okay then, Tonto, let's rock!' she said, grinning behind her own mask and feeling a rush of confidence ride in on her wave of arousal.

When Lukas threw open the doors and positioned himself just behind her and to the side, she took a deep breath and strode straight in, her head held high.

The seating was arranged in a circle again, and this time, a trestle was set in the centre. Glancing around the assembled faces of what were now her peers, Clover studiously avoided looking at the naked man who was fastened across the trestle, face down and trembling. Beyond him across the circle, Clover saw Olivia giving her a look of encouragement, while beside her, the grinning Circe reached across to give her friend's exposed breast a vigorous squeeze.

'Good evening, Mistress Clover,' said a familiar voice, and Clover turned towards the smiling face of Francis Black.

'We're delighted that you could join us,' the older man went on, his eyes raking her from head to foot and glowing warm in a way that said she met with his approval. 'And may I say how impressive you're looking.'

Firmly quashing any naive, enthusiastic expressions of thanks, Clover gave him a grave, contained nod, as elegantly as she could.

'As you see, there's a small matter we're hoping you can deal with for us.' He made an expansive gesture towards the prone and shackled Nathan. 'If that's not too much trouble?'

'I'd be glad to oblige,' murmured Clover, keeping her voice soft and cool, and her expression impassive, just the way Lukas always did.

'And, of course, we have a wide selection of implements for you to choose from.'

Clover permitted herself a narrow smile. 'Thanks very much, but I've brought my own.' Turning to Lukas, she snapped her fingers and nodded towards his waist. Nodding back at her, he deftly unbuckled his fearsome belt and handed it to her.

A mutter of approval and admiration passed around the circle.

The long, heavy strip of leather already felt familiar in her hands and she coiled it confidently around her right one, pausing only to heft its weight just once, as if she were saying hello to an old and favoured friend.

She turned back towards Francis Black and looked him squarely in the eye.

'Do I have the permission of this assembly to begin?' she asked haughtily.

'With the greatest of pleasure. Please proceed.'

Taking up her stance, Clover thought how unimpressive Nathan's behind looked when compared to Lukas's. But even so, the expanse of flesh enticed her, and she felt her clitoris stir beneath the tight crotchpiece of her costume. Sensing the presence of her beloved a couple of yards away to her left, and feeling his strength and skill flow up through her fingers as if had been stored in the belt, she raised her arm, let instinct take her, and sent the leather flying.

As the thunder crack split the air, and Nathan screamed, she allowed herself another little smile.

CHAPTER

15

He was a pretty boy, his features rather delicate, but beneath his sharp, designer suit, Clover sensed his body was toned and strong, and up for anything. She felt a tiny pang of guilt to be checking out this handsome young yuppie she'd been seated next to, rather than focusing solely on the catwalk, but she was confident that her beloved would understand. It was all in a good cause, and he'd ultimately benefit from it too.

As if thought summoned reality, she glanced up to the end of the runway, close to the giant logo – Olivia Foxe in a stylish, looped script – to see a spectacular creature emerge from behind the screening curtains.

As Lukas strolled down the catwalk, there was the customary gasp. He was wearing a dark, fluidly designed suit from Olivia's new menswear collection, and as ever he elevated it from a mere item of clothing to a veritable work of art. His eyes were cool as he scanned the assembled fashionistas with his impassive thousand-yard stare, but when his gaze skimmed over

Clover, she detected his flicker of acknowledgement.

She wondered what the young man beside her would think if he knew that last night Lukas had fucked her while she was in bondage. That the sensational body that held everyone spellbound had laboured naked between her thighs, bringing her to orgasm after dazzling, sweating orgasm.

'He's quite something, isn't he?' she murmured to her new friend.

They were the first words she'd spoken to him, but he agreed with an eager nod of his head. A second later, he blushed furiously and began to stammer back at her.

'Er . . . yes . . . of course, he's a handsome man, but I'm . . . um . . . not like that. If you understand? I like women.'

Clover gave him a long look from beneath her lashes, finding his pinkened face even more appealing. She was aware of Lukas returning up the catwalk just a few feet away, not looking directly at her this time, but all the same aware of what she was up to.

'Now that's a shame. I rather like bisexual men. And I happen to know for a fact that *he* swings both ways too.' She nodded toward the tall, departing figure whose pale golden hair glittered beneath the lights.

'Really?' said the young man beside her, unable to disguise his interest.

Poor thing, thought Clover, he doesn't know where to look. Five minutes ago, before Lukas had sashayed into the spotlight, her companion had barely glanced at the catwalk. He'd been too busy peering surreptitiously down the front of her Olivia Foxe silk crêpe suit.

'Oh yes, he and I know each other very well,' she purred, leaning close and offering more cleavage to confuse him. 'Would you like to meet him after the show?'

'I . . . er . . . yes, I'd like that,' the young man said, licking his lips and shifting uncomfortably in his seat. Clover wondered what his hard-on was like. Was he big? Like Lukas? Then again, no one was like Lukas . . .

She'd been with plenty of men since she'd been initiated into Francis Black's exclusive group of friends and associates – and enjoyed them all – but no one could quite get to her like her glorious Urban Vampire.

'I'd better introduce myself,' said the young man, visibly excited, 'I'm Martin Felgate. Pleased to meet you.' He held out his hand, and Clover could see that he was shaking.

'My pleasure,' she said, hoping it soon would be. 'I'm Clover Weatherby.'

So much had changed since that fateful and illuminating birthday party of Francis's, thought Clover, allowing her attention to drift now she'd hooked Lukas and herself a treat for the evening ahead.

Oh, she'd been so scared when faced with the prospect of her first performance as a dominatrix. But with Lukas's silent support, she hadn't revealed it to the assembled company. And once she'd struck the first blow, she'd loved it!

Nathan had howled; she'd turned his bottom crimson and had received an ovation. With one nod from Francis Black, she'd known she was accepted, part of the group.

The birthday party afterwards had been lavish, and the gifts he'd bestowed phenomenal. And appropriate.

To Olivia he'd given a massive injection of cash for her business, which had led to her current success. On

Circe, he'd bestowed a work of art she'd long coveted. Even the nervous and chastened Nathan had been given a prestigious new commission for a massive outdoor sculpture to stand in the park of Francis's home.

Clover herself? Well, she'd been given her freedom, in a way. Which amounted to a flat of her own, and funds to sponsor her in the pursuit of any career she chose.

Neither of which she was utilising at the moment. Circumstances had decreed that she enjoy what amounted to a bizarre, sex-filled 'gap' year. And pretty soon, she'd moved out of her own flat to share one with her lover.

Lukas was the only one who'd declined a gift of any kind. And the look he'd exchanged with Francis had more or less confirmed that he'd already got everything he'd wanted.

A huge commotion snapped Clover out of her pleasant memories. Olivia was out on the catwalk, accepting rapturous plaudits for what had been a truly fabulous collection. She smiled and waved at Clover as she strode down the catwalk on Lukas's arm, then gave her erstwhile protégée a wink when she noticed Martin Felgate at her side. Lukas himself remained as neutral as ever. Only Clover could interpret the dark twinkle in his eyes.

'Let's get out of here,' she said to her young companion later, as they were circulating and sipping champagne at the after-show party.

'But I thought you were going to introduce me to Lukas?' he protested.

Clover looked him up and down. He looked warm,

nervous, and not too sure of himself, but when she glanced at his crotch, she saw he was sporting a quite respectable hard-on.

Good, she thought, then stroked his damp cheek caressingly.

'All in good time,' she murmured, leading him from the throng.

The show had been held in a five-star hotel – which was owned by Francis Black, she suspected – and not far from the reception room where the party was, Clover had scoped out a small, discreet cloakroom. She led Martin into it, and quickly locked the door behind them.

His brown eyes widened, and he grinned. Clover grinned back. Her new friend clearly thought he was up for anything, but he might get a surprise at what she had in store for him. Closing the gap between them, she slid her hand behind his head and brought his mouth to hers, parting his lips immediately and snaking her tongue between them. At the same time, she dropped her other hand to his crotch and explored his erection with practised fingers through his trousers.

She felt his exclamation of surprise and shock against her mouth but ignored it. Kissing him harder than ever, she deftly unfastened his trousers and slid her hand inside his boxer shorts. His cock was substantial, hot, and hard as rock. It pulsed appealingly, as she assessed its length and texture.

'Hey! Steady on!' he gasped, as she allowed his mouth its freedom while her fingers still contained and measured his manhood.

She gave him a look. *The* look. The cool, steely stare that made even Lukas tremble.

'Be silent,' she said softly, taking his cock by its tip and squeezing it threateningly. Then she drew it out so that it poked out rudely from his clothing, mute evidence of the power she had over him.

'Touch yourself,' she ordered, watching the fear and desire flare equally in his eyes. He opened his mouth to protest again, but thought better of it. His right hand dropped to his penis and curled around it.

'That's right. Now stroke yourself. Make yourself harder. But be careful. If you come, I'll leave immediately.'

Eyes enormous, and mouth slightly agape, he obeyed her, stroking his cock as if it were some wild beast that might attack him at any moment. Clover didn't reveal her emotions, but she smiled inside. He really did have a nice dick, and she'd been dead right about his suitability for her purposes. Her standing in the group would rise even higher if she could induct a choice, new slave.

As Martin began to sigh, his hips bucking slightly, there came a knock at the door. A familiar pattern that Clover recognised, and her inner smile widened and her sex clenched in anticipation.

Martin's face was a mask of horror, and he began to scrabble at his flies, trying to stuff his swollen cock between them.

'No! Stay just as you are. Continue what you were doing.'

His moist mouth formed the 'b' of 'but' and yet he still complied with her instructions, shaking all over as he began to masturbate again.

Clover released the door lock and allowed the person who knocked to enter. And to kiss her deeply as the flabbergasted Martin looked on.

'Great show, lover,' she purred when she and Lukas broke apart.

'Thanks, darling,' he murmured, hands sliding possessively over her hips and thighs, then beneath the short skirt of her designer suit, drawing it upwards.

Clover moaned when he touched her sex. She wore no underwear. She rarely did these days. With a lover like Lukas around, it always paid to be ready and available. Leaning against him, she felt his free arm snake around her.

'You! Don't stop!' she said crisply to her new slave, whose hand had fallen still on his swollen organ. 'This is nothing to do with you. You'll do as you're told.'

As Lukas's fingertips explored and rubbed and circled, Clover felt her head go light and fill with exotic images.

In one she saw Martin, hers to command, hanging naked in chains, his bottom furiously red and his cock equally so. His flesh was bound in straps, release denied it, doubly tormented . . .

In another, he was bent over a chair while Lukas sodomised him with a slow, artistic ruthlessness, his superb body thrusting gracefully and his beautiful face contorted. All around them, their friends in the group watched with interest and glee . . .

In a third picture, she imagined her new slave crouched between her thighs, licking diligently while Lukas kissed her lips and caressed her breasts . . .

As her pleasure gathered, and her clitoris leaped beneath her lover's long, sure fingers, Clover glanced across at Martin and saw his hands flying over his flesh, his hips jerking and his semen spurting.

Oh, you'll suffer for that, my boy, she told him

silently, the very idea of what she might do to him bringing on her own climax, swift and fiery and knee-weakening.

Yes, we'll have such fun together, fun like you'd never believe, she thought happily, feeling Lukas's strong arm embrace her as she flew.